THE WITNESS TREE

THE WITNESS TREE

Lauran Paine

CHIVERS
THORNDIKE

This Large Print edition is published by BBC Audiobooks Ltd, Bath, England and by Thorndike Press®, Waterville, Maine, USA.

Published in 2003 in the U.K. by arrangement with the author c/o Golden West Literary Agency.

Published in 2003 in the U.S. by arrangement with Golden West Literary Agency.

U.K. Hardcover   ISBN 0–7540–7382–3 (Chivers Large Print)
U.K. Softcover   ISBN 0–7540–7383–1 (Camden Large Print)
U.S. Softcover   ISBN 0–7862–5677–X (Nightingale)

The text of this Large Print edition is unabridged.
Other aspects of the book may vary from the original edition.

Set in 16 pt. New Times Roman.

Printed in Great Britain on acid-free paper.

British Library Cataloguing in Publication Data available

Library of Congress Cataloging-in-Publication Data

Paine, Lauran.
    The witness tree / Lauran Paine.
       p.   cm.
    ISBN 0–7862–5677–X (lg. print : sc : alk. paper)
    1. Large type books. I. Title.
PS3566.A34W58 2003
813'.54—dc21   2003055977

CHAPTER ONE

THE BEAR-CAVE

There had been one day of cold wind which alternately swirled in from the north and from the northeast, followed by two days of utter stillness beneath a thickening and motionless low grey sky, and finally three days of deluge which by the second day had brought most of the creeks up out of their beds, had rolled boulders down brushy sidehills, and made life miserable for creatures which were unable to find shelter or which were not insulated against constant soaking, which most creatures were not.

Then the sun came out, the sky was flawlessly blue, steam rose, even up through the mountains and the foothills; and down across the Brulé Valley grass sprang out of the soil.

The three men who had come through the storm by living in a big, smelly bear cave above the foothills partway up through the big timber, came out on the morning the sun shone, considered the immensity of Brulé Valley, considered the miles of rugged northward country where tiers of timber hid the sky and darkened the rocky earth. Then one of them went down to the brawling, swollen creek to take an all-over bath and shave, while the other two went searching for the horses they had not seen since the storm struck. They went with carbines in their fists and sixguns around their waists.

All three of them were spare, weathered, hard-eyed men whose soiled, stained and rumpled clothing suggested that they had probably not looked any cleaner nor more presentable before the storm drove them to search until they'd found the bear cave. But they itched now and they hadn't itched before. As Cal Hunter said, the bear cave was as full of fleas as most bear caves were, and he had elected to itch a little rather than to stand outside, get drenched and probably catch pneumonia.

They had food, spare horseshoes, three boxes each of sixgun and saddlegun ammunition, a change of clothing, and razors. They also had nine thousand dollars in crisp greenbacks which someone had divided into three little packets, each packet containing thirty one hundred dollar greenbacks. Somewhere upon the far side of the thick, vast, and nearly impenetrable mountains, they also had six heavily-armed horsemen on their back-trail; so far back, Jack Brunner said, after he had bathed and shaved and was ready to eat again, that even if the storm hadn't obligingly washed out all trace of their back-trail, those possemen probably could not have been able to stay on it anyway, because of unfordable mountain streams.

The horses had not strayed far. There was a small park about a mile-and-a-half westerly. They had gone over there to crop grass, and judging from the sign when Cal and Hugh found them, they had lasted out the storm beneath immense fir trees whose close-spaced branches and thick needles had taken all the sting out of the raindrops before they ever got down where the horses had patiently stood.

They cooked just beyond the mouth of the cave and used only dry hardwood. They drank and washed at the creek a couple of hundred yards southeast of their bear cave, and they considered Brulé Valley, which they had been able only to dimly make out when the storm drove them down through here seeking shelter. In sunlight the valley looked immense, and it was. As part of an almost endless high-country plateau it ran east and west toward a very dim merging with mountains, and it also went southward until it fetched up against more mountains which could have been a continuation of the easterly and westerly mountains, and if this were so, then the valley was a thousand-mile punchbowl.

But the geography was only of secondary interest to Brunner, Hunter, and Hugh Cole. In the lower, southeasterly far distance there was a town. All they could make out even in that glass-clear atmosphere, was that there were pitched rooftops out there. They could not even make out the roads leading into and out of that town. They had no idea what it was called, but then for that matter they did not know they were upon the fringe of Brulé Valley. They were Montanans. Even Hugh, who had told his companions he had worked south of Wyoming, did not know exactly where they were.

It did not bother the three men. At least up until now it had not been important to them. All they'd worried about up until the storm had washed out their back-trail, was staying in the saddle night and day, putting as much country as possible between them and the bank in northern Montana where they had picked up that three thousand dollars each which was at this time in three separate saddlebags inside the cave.

Hugh's very dark brown eyes scarcely moved as he studied Brulé Valley. 'It's still Wyoming,' he said. 'I don't think they got these big punchbowl valleys down in Colorado.'

Cal Hunter wagged his head. 'I think we got out of Wyoming when we came through those mountains,' he said. 'Three weeks of it— Wyoming isn't that big. I think we're down in Colorado.'

Jack Brunner reached inside his shirt to scratch as he said, 'I don't care if it's New Mexico. You see those rooftops? There's a

4

roominghouse down there where a man can sleep up off the ground, and a place where he can buy a big steak and fried spuds and maybe even blueberry pie, and a saloon where he don't have to worry about fleas.'

Jack was a bull-necked, blue-eyed man with a slightly hooked nose and a granite jaw. He had the physique of an oaken beer barrel. He was shrewd, tough, a little mean, and had a unique sense of humour. Like his companions, he had ridden cattle ranges most of his mature life, and before that had briefly been a blacksmith. Also like Cole and Hunter, he had never fled ahead of a posse before because he had never robbed a bank before. But Jack Brunner and his companions were as thoroughly in their element as outlaws as they had formerly been as rangemen.

The hardship was nothing new; none of them had ever lived without hardship. And the harrowing days balancing along cliff edges, as well as the long, cold and sleepless nights were neither new to them nor novel. The only real difference between rangemen who worked the ranges and rangemen who pointed their guns at bank clerks was in what they did, but everything else was the same— they rode hard, lived hard, faced danger almost every day of their lives, and were inured to every conceivable variety of privation and inconvenience.

Now of course Cole, Brunner and Hunter

had added a fresh dimension to their existences; they were hunted men. Probably by now back up in Montana the people whose indignation would inspire them to do such a thing, would have posted a big reward for all three of them.

For the past three weeks of flight, while resting the horses in some miserable, windy high-mountain dry-camps, they had discussed their new status; and by now as they stood in pleasant sunshine admiring the size and magnificence of Brulé Valley without having any idea it had a name, or where it was, or what that distant town was called, they could look ahead with hopeful expectation because they no longer had to worry about their back-trail. Whatever discomfort that savage storm had caused them—primarily the damned fleas—it had for a fact favoured them more than it had bothered them.

But they did not saddle up and bust down across the huge valley to the distant town. After three weeks of learning to be fugitives they were now thinking like fugitives. They made twig-traps, snared seven sagehens, which were about the dumbest birds the Good Lord ever made, and they had plenty of cold branch water. The horses had that park to the west a ways, and the sun came up each day as shiny as new money; and Cal Hunter who always wanted to be a little lazy, had in fact the seeds in him to be that if he'd ever had the

6

opportunity, told his partners as far as he was concerned they could spend a couple of weeks right where they were, he wouldn't mind at all and neither would the horses.

But Hugh, who was a lanky, high-cheek-boned individual, and the most fastidious of the three, made his unalterable judgment. 'Two more days at the most. It's not that I ain't ready to loaf it's those gawddamned fleas!'

Jack agreed. 'I wouldn't mind stayin' here for a spell, but the darned fleas . . . What do you expect they live on? I don't think a bear's denned up in here in a couple of years. Maybe they bite each other.'

Jack relaxed against a rough-barked fir tree and fished around for his tobacco sack. It was depleted, and the countryside which provided plump sagehens would not re-fill the tobacco sack, so he sighed and said, 'All right. In a couple of days. I'd sort of like to see a pool hall again, anyway, and a stove-cooked meal. All right . . . In a couple of days.'

CHAPTER TWO

THE TRAIL AHEAD

The day after the decision was made to loaf another couple of days Cal Hunter arose at sunrise and went outside to pee, and while he was standing off a ways scratching and peering around puffy-eyed, tawny movement in some nearby wild grape bushes caught his attention. He scarcely breathed for five seconds; he had left his gun and shellbelt atop the bedroll inside the cave. He was as defenceless as a baby. He could have called out. Instead he finished what he had walked out there for, pretended to be admiring the newday brilliance, and waited a long time to catch sight of that tawny movement again.

It was not a man, he was confident of that, and it was neither a bear—it was too light-coloured—nor a deer—it was too close to the ground and thick for that. He speculated that a wolf had been stalking the cave, but he'd never known wolves to linger where they'd picked up strong, fresh man-scent.

Then it moved again, stealthily, and Cal squinted his eyes, stood absolutely motionless, and saw first, the somewhat broad, medium-length nose, then a pair of wide-spaced dark eyes, and finally the broad, rather flat head of a dog.

The animal was rusty taffy colour, had a powerful neck which sloped into massive shoulders. It was neither a young nor old dog; Cal guessed he was perhaps five or six years old. What he was doing up there, was anyone's guess, but Cal thought he was probably a deer-chasing dog, which stockmen shot on sight. Then Cal considered something else: Where had he come from? Neither he nor his two partners had done much exploring, beyond looking over that grassy park where the horses were recovering from much hard use. But that dog, Cal told himself, was not wild, and if he had been lost, or had strayed from that distant town, he would have been more tucked-up than he seemed to be, and he might also have been sore-footed.

Cal began quietly talking. The dog remained in the underbrush watching without making a sound or moving. As a boy back in Missouri Cal Hunter had had a 'yaller' dog like this one, but not quite as muscled-up. He remembered that dog, very fondly, as he slowly sank to one knee and continued to talk. The dog neither fled nor approached, he watched Cal's every move. Then, eventually, he pulled back slightly and turned. In the very next instant he was gone.

Cal went over through the bushes but did not so much as catch a glimpse of the dog again, even though the bushes ended and the forest began over where there was no underbrush.

He went thoughtfully back to the cave where Jack and Hugh were eating cold sagehen, and recounted his experience. Both his companions listened as they finished eating and wiped greasy lingers on their britches' legs, then Hugh said, 'We better look around.'

They did, taking carbines with them, and scattering out as they went along the downward slope of their mountainside. They had seen no buildings of any kind out across that huge valley, except the ones comprising the distant town. It had not occurred to them to consider the foothills immediately below their timbered sidehill. There were trails of different kinds of trees in the lower places throughout those foothills, but elsewhere there was not even very much underbrush, just grass. And perhaps because those foothills were so close, directly below their mountain hideout, and the immensity of Brulé Valley had held their attention, it had not occurred to them there might be buildings in the foothills.

There were. But they were neither very prepossessing to gaze upon, as extensive as a cow-ranch set of buildings ordinarily were, nor particularly noticeable because the logs had been weathered to blend perfectly with the dull colours of the hills themselves.

Where the three of them came together back a few tiers of trees from where brilliant morning sunlight limned those buildings against the very dark green of trees which seemed to be following a meandering watercourse, Jack Brunner knelt, leaned upon his Winchester and drily said, 'Less than a couple of miles from the bear-cave, and we was feelin' as safe as ticks up there.'

They did not see the dog. In fact they did not see anything at all except for someone's brindle milk-cow grazing her way serenely along the creek-side where good grass grew out about a hundred feet on both sides, and one horse standing in a big pole corral, still dozing as fresh sunlight worked the warmth down under his hide.

Cal said, 'Homesteader.'

No one disputed that but they were rangemen who thought as rangemen, so Hugh waved his arm. 'Where are his cattle?'

There was no sign of livestock even out beyond the foothills where that immense punchbowl of a valley began and seemed to flow endlessly.

'Someone's down there,' stated Cal. 'That's a saddlehorse in the corral, an' whether he's got cattle now or not he's sure got a big network of cattle corrals.'

Hugh also knelt and leaned on his saddlegun studying the buildings. 'Old,' he said. 'If he's a squatter he's been here a long time. Those buildings are old.'

Cal had satisfied part of his curiosity as he

11

shoved up to his feet and slung the Winchester in the crook of one arm. 'He hasn't had cattle in a long time. Look how high the weeds are in those corrals nearest the back of the log barn. Hasn't been no grazing animals in there in a spell . . . Well hell, now that we know he's down there, and his yaller dog knows we're up at the bear-cave . . .'

No one finished it for Cal as they started back to camp. It was time to move on anyway. One more day of lying over, or one less day, did not make any difference—not as long as the sun was shining.

They checked the twig-snares on their way, found three more plump sagehens, and when they got back to camp leaned aside the saddleguns to sit in the shade talking and plucking feathers.

'Straight south,' stated Jack Brunner. 'We're goin' to hit Arizona directly.'

Hugh thought about that. 'All I ever heard about Messico was that it's hotter'n hell, and the people will steal the boots off your feet when you're wide awake.'

Jack shrugged. 'First we got to go through that town yonder, get new shoes put on the horse all around, get our hair sheared, maybe eat a decent meal and belly up to a bar.'

No one argued about that, but in the back of each man's mind there was a tingle of warning. Still, they were a very considerable distance from northern Montana.

Cal looked up smiling a little. 'You know, when I was growin' up I had a yaller dog pretty much like that one. One hell of a dog, but most of all he was my best friend. We lived out; there wasn't no other kids to play with. I used to run a trap line in winter, and hunt the canebrakes in summer. That dog could think like a man, so help me.'

Cole held up his sage chicken, without its leathers it still looked fat. He brushed at some blue-tailed flies which came near, lowered the bird and eased his hat forward to keep what little sun-brilliance which touched the clearing in front of their cave from bothering his eyes. Hugh Cole was a breed. He was less than half Indian, but he still showed that he was a breed. He did not use tobacco and although he drank a little, he had never been drunk in his life. He had been raised at one of those Agency missionary schools. He had been a good student. In fact lanky, tall Hugh Cole was more than adaptable, he excelled at whatever he did. But at times he would turn reticent and since both his partners knew this, when he chose not to talk they left him alone.

Now though, he was in an easy and relaxed mood as he said, 'I had a dog . . . My paw disappeared one springtime and never came back. My maw was three-quarters Assiniboin. She put me in a church school and went back to her people in Canada.'

This was more personal information than

13

Hugh had ever volunteered before and it interested both his companions. Cal said, 'What happened to your dog?'

Hugh slapped at more blue-tailed flies. 'Couldn't keep him at the school. I tried like hell to find someone who'd want him. He wasn't a pretty dog, and he'd fight other dogs, and once he bit a preacher at the school . . . I don't know what happened to him. He just turned up missin' and I never saw him again.'

Jack Brunner growled. 'Someone shot him,' he said, and perhaps because Hugh had long thought this was so, he nodded his head. Then he arose and went over to feed twigs into their fire-ring. With his back to them he said, 'I know . . . dogs that chase deer will chase cattle and maybe even kill little calves. I know the rule about that . . . but I never shot a dog in my life.' For a moment he was quiet as he coaxed a tiny blue flame to life beneath the tipi of small dry twigs, then he also said, 'I've never seen a dog I couldn't get along with . . . but I sure can't say as much for some of the sons of bitches who've owned dogs.'

That was true enough. Cal and Jack did not comment but they agreed. Like all men who lived close to animals in big country, they had had more laughs over animal behaviour than over human behaviour. They liked and understood animals; that went with being stockmen. They had always attributed a reasoning process to animals. They could tell

14

stories all night long of how some old mossback cow with a baby calf had outsmarted them in the underbrush, or how a staggy steer had turned invisible when he had seen horsemen approaching, or how a brave old bull had waited like a stone statue until he had measured the distance a man walked away from his saddlehorse in open country, and had charged the man when he knew the man could not get back to his horse quickly enough.

When Hugh had the fire burning with an intense flame, he went after some green twigs for them to spit the birds upon. The afternoon was wearing along, what little light came down into the timber around the cave and its grassy opening, was slanting and dusty-seeming.

Cal went back to look at the horses, Jack went down to the creek for an all-over bath—only the Lord knew when he'd get another one—and Hugh wiped sagehen grease off his hands with swathes of pulled grass, then tipped back his hat to study as much of the sky as was visible; there was not a cloud up there. It would not rain, at least into the foreseeable future, and that was important to men riding across open country.

When Cal returned he thought it over for a long time before going down to the creek for an all-over bath too. He might not have done it except for the fleas, and even then, by the time he got back to camp, the confounded little varmints were biting him again; so as he sank

15

down in disgust for his last smoke of the day, he said tomorrow when they reached that town he was going to the general store and buy everything new from the hideout, and burn his old attire, and the damned fleas along with it.

Hugh had been thinking ahead while his partners had been absent from camp. Now, he said, 'If we're in Colorado, then by my calculations we got to be maybe a little more'n half way down toward New Messico, and in my geography books in school, if we angled more southwesterly we'd ought to be able to save a lot of miles and get over into Arizona. After that, hell, we'll be so far from upper Montana we could lie over for a spell before headin' on down into Messico . . . and for all I know, maybe we could stay in Arizona.'

Jack exhaled blue smoke as he considered all this. 'I rode with a feller once who'd come from Arizona. He said once you hit the desert country down there, it's just like Messico, except that they got better cattle. He also said if you can't talk Spanish, even in Arizona, you got a handicap.'

This topic faded. Hugh was the only one of them who had any idea that they might be able to cut miles off the trip if they changed course. Generally, all Cal and Jack knew about the southern cattle country was that it did not snow much in wintertime. They'd been hearing that for many years when many seasonal rangemen headed out of Montana to get away from the rigorous, bitterly cold winters.

Cal was perfectly agreeable to altering course. He was one of those people who rarely bucked destiny. He also had an almost fatalistic variety of patience, and right now whether they rode due south to find Mexico, or angled off a little to save time while still heading for Mexico, did not interest him as much as the lure of that distant town. Nor was he thinking exclusively of getting rid of his flea-infested, worn-out clothing either. Cal had always been a man who looked forward to Saturday when it was customary for rangeriders to head for a town.

Hugh shortened his perspective as he leaned in the warm gloaming and said, 'We're goin' to look pretty damned mangy—long hair, dirty old clothes, ridden-down horses, scraggly beards.'

If that had been said as a mild warning Jack Brunner did not worry about it. 'I've come in off roundups after bein' out for two, three months, lookin' just as bad an' smellin' a hell of a lot worse,' he said, and stood up to stretch and scratch as he eyed the big opening of the bear-cave. 'In a way I sort of hate to leave this camp.'

Jack snorted. The hidden parts of his hide were evidently more sensitive to flea bites than the hides of his partners. He gazed sourly at the cave opening. 'No sir, I'm glad to be leavin' and after this if I can smell bear in a cave I'll

17

sleep outside even if it's rainin' cats and dogs.'

Hugh, who did not smile often, drifted his gaze around to Jack Brunner's powerful body in the deepening gloom, and grinned. But he said nothing.

They dragged their saddlery outside where it would be handier in the morning, then went into the cave's utter darkness to grope for their bedrolls.

After they had all been bedded down for a while Jack suddenly said, 'Y'know, if we got to keep this up, and was to set down with a pencil and paper and figure it out, I doubt if that three thousand dollars each of us got would amount to much more than tophand wages for the same length of time.'

'Except,' stated Hugh, as he rolled up onto his side, 'this way we got it all in one chunk. The other way we'd pee it away a dollar at a time, and after the same length of time had passed, we still wouldn't have anything . . . You know what you could do with that three thousand dollars, Jack? Find a nice little cow outfit down south somewhere, buy it for cash, and never have to work for anyone else as long as you live.'

After that, nothing more was said.

CHAPTER THREE

HAMMERSVILLE

The town was called Hammersville, and the rotund dayman at the liverybarn had a standard joke he made of that for the benefit of strangers.

'A feller name of Asa Dunning first settled Brulé Valley. He came out of Nebraska with a bunch of cattle. There was a big fight with some In'ians he come onto. He ran 'em off—him and his riders—but them In'ians killed Dunning's favourite saddlehorse, a critter Dunning called Hammerhead. In honour of his horse old Dunning named the settlement he founded right in this spot, after that horse. It's been Hammersville ever since.'

Like most people who had to get their two-bits' worth in first, the paunchy dayman was too busy telling his story to pay much attention to the unkempt appearance of the three men listening to him, and even after they had paid in advance for their horse care and had trooped all together toward the general store, he could not have given much of a description of them.

But the storekeeper could have. He outfitted all three of them with new shirts, britches, underpants, socks, and the one his

19

friends called Cal had bought a new hat and a blue neckerchief. He was the man who told the storekeeper to burn their old clothing because it was full of fleas, and that had made an impression, so the storekeeper had wasted no time in obeying.

The poker-faced proprietor of the tonsorial parlour had shorn and shaved the same three men, and had charged them ten cents each for the use of his bath-house out back. The price included a chunk of strong brown soap and three threadbare towels.

By the time they reached the only café in Hammersville, a lot of their uniqueness had vanished, and after eating heartily and paying up, the day was also waning. They strolled up to the roominghouse first, got a big room with three wall-bunks in it, then returned to the centre of town on their way to the saloon.

They took a bottle and three glasses to a far table, eased down, stretched out, and savoured their first raw whiskey in a very long time, but it had little effect after all the food they had eaten.

Jack was mellow. 'It's a nice town,' he said, and gazed at the sprinkling of customers in the saloon. 'We could maybe loaf here for a spell.'

Both Hugh and Jack turned toward Brunner without speaking, and as he sighed and leaned to re-fill his glass, a pair of dusty rangemen walked in heading for the bar, and directly behind them came a thick, large man with a badge on his shirt-front. Three sets of eyes watched the large lawman go over and lean beside the pair of cowboys to order his drink and strike up a conversation with the riders, totally unaware that he was the object of some intense, but veiled, interest.

Cal said, 'I've never known many of those bastards that I cared much for, but this is the first time I ever saw one an' felt the hair under my hat rise up.'

Jack Brunner reached for the bottle. 'Get used to it,' he said, and re-filled his glass, then shoved the bottle across to Hugh, but Cole had already had his drink and made no move to have another one.

Drily alluding to Jack's earlier comment about loafing in Hammersville, Hugh Cole said, 'You want to head out in the morning, Jack?'

He got no answer until after Brunner had finished his drink and had blinked back some tears. 'Yeah. Not much point in wastin' time anyway.'

Hugh's dark eyes brightened with sardonic humour, and a moment later a wispy older man wearing a wrinkled suit-coat walked into the saloon, his shapeless hat tipped back as he headed for the bar wearing a bleak look. The large lawman turned casually away from the rangeriders he had been conversing with and looked down at the smaller and older man. 'You look like something just bit you,' he said.

21

The older man nodded to the passing barman then twisted slightly toward the lawman. In a brittle, disapproving voice he said, 'You know, Ben, I've tried likin' old Shultz and his riders. I've patched and splinted 'em, and have treated Walt Shultz for his heart condition for I suppose close to ten years now . . . But today it came to me I been engagin' in a losing fight.'

The lawman continued to regard his agitated, older friend from a smooth, placid countenance. 'What happened?'

'You recollect those young folks who moved in up at old Hatrack Hanson's place in the foothills northwest of town?'

'Yeah. His granddaughter and her husband. What about them?'

'One of Walt Shultz's blow-hard cowboys shot their dog this morning.'

The lawman's expression did not alter. 'Shot their dog . . .'

The wiry, smaller man downed his whiskey and shook his head when the bartender would have re-filled the glass. 'Yes. Rode into their yard and when the dog did what any decent dog would do—walked into the yard and barked, the cowboy shot him. Never said a word, just drew and shot the dog.'

'Well, he'd have a reason, Frank.'

The smaller man lifted shrewd, sceptical eyes. 'Ben, he did not say a word, and after he shot the dog he turned his horse and rode out of the yard. That's all there was to it.'

The big lawman leaned down atop the bar, thought a moment, then said, 'Maybe he figured the dog was goin' to bite him, or snap at his horse's rear feet, or—'

The older man's anger exploded. 'So— suppose some man walks in here today and thinks you're going to shoot him—and don't even open his mouth, just ups and shoots you first.'

The big lawman became placating. 'Frank, you're a good doctor, you've pulled a lot of people through a lot of different things . . . Frank, it was just a dog, wasn't it; he didn't threaten old Hatrack's granddaughter or her husband, did he?'

The wizened, weathered face of the medical practitioner reddened. Clearly, age and small size notwithstanding, he was a man of temper. 'It was just a dog,' he spat out, mimicking the sheriff. 'Sure, it was just a dog, and the last time one of Walter Schultz's swaggering loudmouths did something, it was that milk cow those homesteaders had up along Buffalo Creek. Same thing—rode in, didn't say a word, shot the cow and rode out.' The doctor's small, faded eyes were fixed harshly upon the lawman. 'What did you do that time, Ben?'

The lawman continued to lean atop the bar, but to Cal, Hugh and Jack who were sitting nearby listening, it was clear that the sheriff was beginning to bristle. He did not turn his

23

head when he softly said, 'Like I said, Frank, you're a good doctor, and seems to me that ought to take up most of your time. Why don't you just stay with that and keep out of other things.'

For a moment it appeared that the angry medical practitioner would lash out, and that would have been a mistake; he was less than half the weight and heft of the larger man, and was probably twenty-five years older. After a long struggle, the doctor said, 'Ben, I'm going to tell you something else; I've tried to see your side of a lot of things too. I've liked you part of the time, but right now that's very hard to do.' He slammed down some silver beside his empty glass and stamped out of the saloon.

The heavy-set, fleshy barman came along, gazed impassively past at the quivering doors, then pulled his gaze back to the sheriff. 'What was all that about?'

The sheriff straightened up slightly wagging his head. 'Oh, you know how Frank Tillitson is; always takin' up for some damned poor cause. This time it's the girl and her man out at Hatrack's old homestead in the foothills. Someone shot their damned dog.'

The barman made an automatic swipe over the bartop where the doctor's sticky glass had been, and looked more bored than concerned when he replied. 'Schultz'll get 'em out of there. That skinny feller never spends a dime in here when they come to town. That's the trouble with settlers—they don't help the community worth a damn.'

The big lawman turned slightly, saw three freshly shaved and shorn, lined and bronzed rangemen in new attire looking steadily at him. For a moment he appraised them, then he wagged his head and walked out of the saloon.

Jack Brunner rolled and lit a smoke. 'For a little old man that pill-roller's got bottom to him. I figured he was goin' to take a swing at the lawman.'

Cal was re-reading the label on their bottle when he said, 'You can smell it when you ride into one of these cow towns. They're closed. Chris' himself could come ridin' in here on that burro Joseph was leadin' and they use buggy whips on 'em.' He raised dark eyes. 'I took a lot of pay from 'em, rode their horses and worked the cattle, so maybe I hadn't ought to be sayin' this—but there are a lot of pure sons of bitches who own big cow outfits.'

His partners could agree with that, and they did, but perhaps because of a twinge of conscience, Cal Hunter finally mitigated the condemnation a little.

'Well hell, you get 'em in every line of work. Blacksmiths, freighters, storekeepers, lawmen—maybe mostly among lawmen—you name it, and they're among 'em.'

Cal shoved the bottle back. He was feeling very comfortable. 'How about some pool? I saw the poolhall across the road when we was walkin' up here. How about two bits a game?'

Jack stared. 'Two bits? You never played for more'n ten cents a game before since I've known you.'

Cal grinned. 'I can afford two bits now. So can you. Come along.'

Outside, the sun was nearly gone, the café was doing a brisk business; down in front of his log jailhouse that big lawman whose first name was Ben, stood in desultory conversation with a couple of cowmen, one of whom walked with an ash cane. He too was big and hefty and bear-like, but he had more age on him than the sheriff.

Cal led the way over to the east side of the wide roadway where it was a little darker than it was on the west side of the road. Behind them, as Hugh Cole stepped up onto the plankwalk, the last of them to do so, four rangemen loped down the centre of the road and in sport one of them reined off to expedite Hugh's stepping up. It was nothing; rangemen did those things to one another, then everyone laughed. But Hugh did not laugh. He turned and gazed at the stranger, watched the man veer back to his companions, then Hugh turned to follow Jack and Cal into the dingy poolhall.

There were three tables and no one was playing at any of them. The proprietor, whose toothpick moved each time he spoke, had the soft pulpy appearance of a man who had

26

avoided work and exercise all his life. He nodded, held out his hand for the coins, then gestured. 'Any table you want.'

Cal was a fair hand with a pool cue, and he had unerring aim, but Cal was an impetuous gamester; whether playing pool for two bits a game or stud poker for a lot more money, he was impulsive.

Jack had never learned to hold back, and because he was a physically very powerful man, occasionally despite his efforts not to cause it, the balls would spring over the railing of the table and bounce along the floor. Today, though, he was being particularly restrained; he had learned from playing against Cal Hunter down the years, that if an adversary of Cal really wanted to win, all he had to do was make Cal a little nervous; then he would take shots in a rush that no sensible person would take.

Hugh, for all his lanky, loose-jointed frame and perfect coordination, just could not shoot a respectable game of pool. He tried, as he was doing now; he concentrated, did not speak, ignored everything except the balls and the table in front of him, and never sank more than two balls straight running. If the frustration this was bound to cause in any man, ever became anger, Hugh never showed it, but then that was a characteristic of Hugh Cole that many people had noticed over the years. He was very good at masking how he really felt.

Despite Jack's clever strategy, Cal won the first game and collected the half dollar this entitled him to. The next game Jack won hands down. He had increased his pressure on Cal and the erratic impulsiveness became so pronounced that Cal missed elementary bank shots four times. And afterwards Cal got red in the face.

The third game was going well for Jack again when Hugh ran up five sinkers in a row, something his partners did not believe he had ever done before, and which, in fact, he had never done before. But Hugh did not smile, did not show any elation. He still played as doggedly as ever.

A group of rangemen came in as the proprietor was trying to make his kerosene lantern fire up. They paid for a table, waited impatiently, finally took the lantern away from the proprietor, got it lighted among the four of them, handed it back and approached the table behind Cal, Jack and Hugh.

Neither group heeded the other. Hugh in particular, on his winning streak, would not have looked up if the President himself had strolled in.

But after sinking his fifth ball in consecutive order, Hugh made a mistake; instead of the cue ball tipping a ball into a pocket less than six inches distant, the cue ball narrowly missed the target, struck the railing and came to a lonely stop.

One of the riders at the adjoining table snickered. For a fact, it had been a shot a child should have been able to make. Hugh straightened up, leaned on his cue stick and did not face around as he watched Jack hunch for a clean shot.

Jack had to make his best showing now or lose to Hugh. He worked his cue-stick, and fired. The ball flew over the slate, struck the far railing, sprang nearly ten inches into the air and crashed to the floor where it rolled beneath the table of the four rangemen who were just beginning their game.

They all stopped, looked down at the ball, turned to gaze at red-faced Jack Brunner, then one of them stooped, picked up the ball, pitched it to Jack and said, 'Mister, you'd ought to stick to dungin' out barns.'

The cowboy had not smiled. He then leaned down to concentrate on his shot, and there was not a sound anywhere throughout the poolhall. Even the proprietor, who had witnessed the act of pure contempt, did not make a sound. He saw those first three pool players, turn, straighten up as they considered the other four men, and the proprietor knew what he should do—run for Sheriff Albright—instead he stood as though glued to the floor.

CHAPTER FOUR

TROUBLE!

The concentrating cowboy was leaning down, his body tensed for his first shot, and precisely at the moment he started to push the cue, Jack dropped his stick and coughed. The combination of noises certainly did not help the pool-shooter, but he may not have done much anyway; without straightening up he lifted his head and looked unblinkingly at Jack Brunner. Jack very distinctly said, 'Mister, you'd ought to stick to dungin' out barns.'

The other faded, hard-bodied rangemen turned, and the leaning man straightened up, his knuckles around the pool-cue bone white.

Some men would have left it there, but Jack continued to gaze at the cowboy as he also said, 'If you can't take rough talk, partner, then you hadn't ought to give it.'

The proprietor was frozen over by his little table. The four riders stood a long while considering Cal, Jack and Hugh. One of them, a loose-jointed, red-headed older man finally said, 'All right, leave it be, Carl.'

The cowboy seemed not to have heard the warning from his red-headed companion. He was looking directly at Jack Brunner when he said, 'In here, mister, or outside?'

Jack's lips drew downward a little. 'You're not goin' to win either way, Mister—take your choice.'

Now, finally, the proprietor had found his voice. He called loudly to the motionless, tense men farther back in his place of business. 'Not in here. I run a respectable business. You fellers come get your money back and go outside.'

No one heeded the frightened, pulpy man. The cowboy facing Jack Brunner jerked his head a little and leaned to slide his cue-stick atop the table. 'Outside.'

Hugh said nothing but Cal eased over beside Jack as the four rangemen put down their sticks and started for the door. 'Weasle out of it,' he said. 'We don't need a week in jail here.'

They started for the door, and as they were departing that bear-like older man who used a cane and who had been talking to the sheriff down in front of the jailhouse an hour or so earlier, came trudging up, and halted. He said nothing, but he looked at the faces of the four rangeriders, particularly at the red-headed man, then turned as the three strangers in new attire also walked out of the poolhall. He got a deep crease between both eyes, and leaned on his cane as he said, 'What's this all about, Red?'

The older rangeman jerked a thumb. 'Carl argued with one of these fellers.'

The bear-like big older man put an intense, hard stare upon Hugh, then upon Cal, and finally upon Jack Brunner. When he spoke the words came out as a gruff growl. 'Who do you fellers ride for?'

None of the three men in doorway shadows answered nor even looked at the older man, they were watching Red and Carl and the other two.

The older man's big fist gripped his cane-handle tightly. Hugh was closest so the older man tapped harshly with his cane when he spoke again. 'Injun, I asked who you fellers ride for!'

Hugh moved just his eyes, regarded the big older man briefly then said, 'Keep out of this, old man.'

Behind, farther back from the doorway, the poolhall proprietor gasped, then spoke up in a reedy way. 'Mister Schultz, they just come in an' was playin' pool . . .'

Walter Schultz speared the pulpy man with one singeing look and turned back toward Hugh Cole again: 'Injun; go get on your horse and keep riding.'

Jack Brunner swore under his breath and started forward toward the man who had ridiculed him. The other three rangemen standing with Carl shifted slightly, and that was when Cal, partially behind Hugh and opposite Walter Schultz drew and cocked his Colt. The ominous cocking sound brought instantaneous halt to all movement, except where men's eyes searched for the threatening gun.

Hugh also drew, but without haste. Then he smiled one of his very rare smiles. 'Eat him up,' he said to Jack Brunner, who only glanced back to see who had cocked the weapon, then started forward again, his full attention riveted upon the cowboy the other rangemen had called Carl.

Walter Schultz leaned heavily upon his cane, mouth pulled flat in an ugly way. But he said no more. For the moment he was content to watch.

Over in front of the saloon some idlers saw what has happening, sprang off their bench and fled inside to yell around the saloon that a fight was starting over in the road out front of the poolhall. In moments the saloon was emptied. Elsewhere, up and down both sides of the roadway spectators appeared as if by magic, and while none offered to walk up closer to the poolhall, every one of them got ranged along the plankwalk or out into the middle of the roadway to watch.

Carl made a dramatic movement by removing his hat and handing it to one of his companions. Jack sneered at that and kept walking. Then Carl raised both fists, forearms close together above his chest, and began moving to one side. Jack Brunner was like a bull. He was built like one and fought like one.

He did not bother to get both feet set when he turned to stay with Carl—and was hit up alongside the temple with a sledging blow that buckled his knees and sent him down on all fours, blinking and hatless.

Carl sprang in with a boot poised. Hugh spoke flatly. 'I'll kill you if you kick him when he's down!'

Carl stopped in mid-motion. Hugh's black eyes were stone-steady. Carl put his booted foot down, then sneered. 'Takes all three of you fellers to fight one man, don't it?'

Hugh did not respond, and as Jack rolled a little to one side to regain his feet, Carl stepped around on that side too, right fist cocked and poised. Jack did not come all the way up; with a roar he catapulted ahead, caught Carl around the middle and carried him at least ten feet before Carl fell backwards with Jack atop him.

Old Schultz grunted loudly but said nothing as Carl struggled frantically to get out of the bear-grip Jack had around him. He tried to hit Jack in the face, but Brunner, who had been here many times before, shoved his face hard into his adversary's chest and the blows were deflected. Then Jack gave one tremendous squeeze, and when Carl's breath pumped out, Jack released him, got upright, and stood with both arms at his side, waiting.

He allowed Carl to scrabble in the manured dirt, allowed him to crab-crawl sideways peering over his shoulder at Jack, and to finally get back upright. But Carl had been hurt. He almost ran to avoid each rush Brunner made, and finally, when Jack's red-rage had worked itself out and he stopped making those lunges, Carl came around him on the left side, moving in the direction of his three motionless friends, and shot a long-arm strike which barely grazed Jack's chest. Then he moved back once more and went in the opposite direction. He had guessed that Jack was not fast on his feet, and he was correct. But he could never have beaten Brunner by those little grazing blows, and after employing them for a short while the old man leaning on his cane growled at him.

'Fight him, damn it all, Carl. *Fight him*!'

Carl was fast, light on his feet, and shifty, but when he started forward and Brunner snarled and acted as though he would catapult himself forward, Carl ran backwards so abruptly that one of his friends made a scornful sound. Then Jack balanced forward and manoeuvred Carl back toward the plankwalk. Each time Carl tried to shift to the left or the right, Jack countered and blocked him. He had done this before too. The moment Carl's heels touched the slightly raised plankwalk he would have to shift stance in order to raise a foot. Behind him Cal and Hugh moved well away and the poolhall proprietor fled deeper into his building.

Carl felt the wood at his heels and leaned to shift his centre of balance before stepping up. Jack went after him with all the speed he was capable of. He caught a stinging left hand along the cheek, then was past that outflung arm. He hit Carl over the heart, and as the cowboy staggered, Jack raised his sights, hit Carl three times with unexpected speed around the head, and as Carl stumbled feebly back along the front of the poolhall, the bear-like big old man with the cane growled.

'That's enough!'

Jack still had a man on his feet in front of him and started in again. The old man raised his ash cane to swing it. Hugh flung up a long arm, deflected the cane, kneed the big old man in the left hip, which was Walter Schultz's bad hip, and as the man nearly fell Hugh wrenched away the cane, spun Schultz and broke the ash cane over Schultz's rear.

Carl went down and rolled off the wall sidewards, bleeding at nose and mouth.

Cal missed most of it. When Hugh went after Walter Schultz Cal was left to keep his cocked sixgun on the other three men.

Walter Schultz fell against the poolhall's front wall and the entire building-front shivered. Hugh flung aside the handle of the cane and with black eyes blazing, grasped Schultz by the older man's loose-fitting coat, turned him, and slapped him; did not ball up his fist, but used the flat of his palm. The blow

36

sounded like a firecracker exploding. Men who had been excitedly shouting before, suddenly went silent and remained that way.

Jack found his new hat out in the roadway, beat it against his leg, then stood among the three cowboys, glaring. He did not say a word, he looked at each of them in turn, then walked back into the gloom of the poolhall's wooden overhang, dumped the dented hat upon the back of his head and said, 'Do you fellers work for this old bastard?'

The red-headed man nodded, watching Jack intently.

'And,' snarled Jack, 'his name is Walter Schultz?'

Again the red-headed man nodded his head.

Jack raised one set of raw knuckles to gingerly massage it with his other hand and said, 'Which one of you shot a man's dog up in the foothills today?'

This time no one seemed to be breathing. Not a word was said until Walter Schultz had himself braced against the rough front wall of the poolhall so that he would not collapse, now that he no longer had his cane. He was studying Jack Brunner with eyes as cold as ice. 'Who are you? What's it to you what my men do?'

Hugh answered for Jack. 'Just some fellers who like dogs.'

Jack asked the question again. 'Which one

37

of you shot that dog?'

Finally, a narrow-faced rangeman with a prominent adam's apple, pointed to the battered, unconscious man behind Jack. 'Carl,' he said.

Down at the jailhouse a breathless spectator had burst inside. A moment later that big, beefy lawman was bearing down upon the roadway out front of the poolhall carrying a sawed-off shotgun in the bend of one arm. He did not speak until he was close enough so that he would not have to raise his voice, then he slung the shotgun forward as though to cock it, and both Hugh and Cal Hunter twisted their wrists. Sheriff Albright may not have seen the guns before, but he saw them now and with a thumb resting atop one of the shotgun's twin hammers, did not cock the weapon as he said, 'Put up those guns. What happened here?'

A man over in front of the saloon yelled out, 'That feller with the new hat whipped the hell out'n one of Mister Schultz's cowboys, and it was a fair fight, Sheriff.'

Other men hooted agreement with this. Sheriff Albright turned toward Schultz. 'Are you all right, Walter?'

Schultz was not all right but he kept his mouth tightly closed. Where he had been struck when the cane broke gave him considerable pain, as did his bad hip. All he said was, 'I don't know what started it, but those three saddle-tramps jumped my men out

38

here in the roadway.'

A derisive voice called from among the distant spectators. 'They sure did, Sheriff. Those *three* fellers jumped Mister Schultz's *four* fellers.'

There was a ripple of snickering laughter up and down the roadway.

Sheriff Albright faced Hugh and Cal again. 'I said—put up those guns.'

They obeyed, Jack examined his injured set of knuckles, and when Ben Albright gestured with his shotgun, Jack led off southward in the direction of the jailhouse, Cal and Hugh following.

Across the roadway in deepening shadows that round-faced bartender turned to re-enter the saloon as he said, 'Nothin' but pure luck. That stranger was just plain lucky. I've seen Carl fight. He's had trainin' somewhere. That was just dumb-brute luck.'

A wizened older man with an askew hat and a rumpled suit coat emerged near the saloon doorway and smiled straight into the barman's face. 'If that was luck, Henry, then I'd like to see that stranger go to work on you, just to prove he can't do it again.'

The bartender halted, looked around, considered the wizened older man in hostile silence for a moment, then ploughed ahead into the saloon, and behind him several townsmen grinned. One said, 'Doc, you've got some stitchin' to do on Mister Albright's fightin' cowboy . . . I'll stand you a round.'

Doctor Tillitson hesitated, squinting over where Walter Schultz's men were trying to hold Carl on his feet, and sighed. 'I better go look after the idiot,' he said, and walked across the now deserted, dusk-scented roadway.

Someone had provided big, bear-like and lame Walter Schultz with a pool-cue to make up for his destroyed cane, and he was leaning on it as Doctor Tillitson shouldered rangeriders aside to examine Carl. 'Hold him,' he snapped as two of the rangemen would have stepped clear. 'I don't want him fallin' on me.'

Walter Schultz beckoned to the red-headed man. 'Find out who they are, where they're stayin' and what Ben's goin' to do with 'em. Most of all, find out when he's goin' to turn 'em out.'

The red-headed older rangeman started southward as Frank Tillitson finished his cursory examination and pointed. 'Carry him up to my place, boys,' and as the rangeman started away with the barely conscious fighter Tillitson turned on Walter Schultz. 'Broken nose, maybe a broken jaw, and I think some cracked ribs.'

Schultz looked down at the doctor. 'Patch him up.'

'He'll have to stay at my place for a few days.'

Schultz snorted. 'Keep the son of a bitch

there for the rest of his life for all I care, Tillitson. He'll never draw another day's pay from me. I'll send someone in with his wages tomorrow.'

'Mister Schultz, he did the best he could do.'

The bear-like larger man fixed Frank Tillitson with a cold stare, 'Runnin' backwards?' Schultz's lips twisted. 'And when my man comes in with Carl's money tomorrow, send me back some more heart pills by him.'

Tillitson regarded the large old man for a while then said, 'And some salve for your behind, Mister Schultz?'

The large man's nostrils flared. 'You get funny with me, Frank, and I'll break your scrawny gawddamned neck. Now get out of my way.'

CHAPTER FIVE

THE HAMMERSVILLE JAILHOUSE

By the time it had all been explained to Sheriff Albright, his expression showed patient disgust. He had been behind a badge for a long time, and if he'd ever had to summarise his opinion about why things like this happened, he would have said it was because men *had* to fight. Otherwise he'd have had to say men were foolish—just because someone had made a slurring remark one man had been beaten very badly, another one had been humiliated in front of the town and would never forget that, and as sure as Ben Albright was sitting there gazing resignedly at what he felt confident was a trio of drifting rangemen— saddle-tramps—Walt Schultz would exact vengeance. Walt had that kind of nature, and along with it, he had the wealth to see to it that when Walt wanted to punish three men or a town, he could do it.

Sheriff Albright had always favoured rangemen; when he had started out in the law business, that was about the only kind of man who covered the ranges, strode the plankwalks, or supported the towns and maintained the kind of law which preceded Ben Albright's kind of law. He still was partial to rangemen. He always would be, but right now he had three rangemen sitting in his office opposite him, and outside of town somewhere, one big, vengeful, influential cowman who would not hesitate for one moment to see that these three saddle-tramps were killed.

He finally said, 'Over a damned pool game.'

Hugh sat like a carving studying the big man. No one had told Sheriff Albright it had also been over a dog.

'Where are you fellers from?'

Cal made an elaborate gesture as he said, 'Most places, Sheriff. We been hiring out to ride a long time, and we've rode every place, just about, that they hire men to ride.'

Ben Albright sighed and leaned on his desktop. 'Where are you heading now?'

Cal answered again, without the elaborateness this time because he felt confident enough to look Albright squarely in the eye while lying to him. 'East. Over to Nebraska, maybe. Or maybe even over as far as Kansas. We heard they got a real big livestock business in the open country over in that direction.'

Ben fixed Cal with an unfriendly eye. 'Did you know who that old man with the cane was?'

They hadn't; all three of them shook their heads.

'But you know now,' said Albright drily. 'He's the biggest cowman in the Brulé Valley

43

country. And he's wealthy and powerful. And Walt Schultz . . . boys, you humiliated him before everyone here in town today. That's never happened before. You shouldn't have done it. You shouldn't have taken his cane away from him.' Ben Albright was gazing steadily at Hugh Cole. 'You can't buck him. You beat one of his men today. Tomorrow he'll hire two more to take that one's place, and if you whip them he'll hire eight more. You see what I mean? You made the worst enemy you'll ever have, today. He'll live to bury all three of you, unless you get out of the valley and put a lot of distance between you'n him.'

Jack had a blue bandana wrapped loosely around his raw right-hand set of knuckles as he slouched on a wall-bench gazing at Sheriff Albright. His original judgement, over at the saloon, had been that Albright was Schultz's man. Now, after listening to Albright, he thought the sheriff was not Schultz's man as much as he was every cowman's defender, and Jack could understand something like that. He too had been favourable to stockmen ever since having become one. He was still sympathetic toward them even though he was no longer one of them—but Ben Albright obviously had no inkling that Jack and his partners had changed professions, were in fact fugitives from men like Ben Albright.

Jack looked at Cal and Hugh; they, like him,

were slouching and relaxed, saying nothing as they gradually came down from that moment of high tension up the road a short while ago. He said, 'Suits me, Sheriff. We was on our way when we rode into your town. Tomorrow we figure to get our horses shod, then be on our way again . . . That wasn't our doing. Those fellers came into the poolhall like they owned it, and turned a little nasty. That's how it started.'

Ben Albright looked as though he accepted that as the truth. Everyone in Hammersville knew what Walt Schultz was like, and how his men acted as a sort of rough reflection of the man who employed them. Ben had been living with it a long time, had learned how to balance between the two factions, and was in fact very adept at it. But in the back of big Ben Albright's mind there was, and had been for a long time, a suspicion that sooner or later, someday, he was going to be unable to maintain that balance. But as he gazed at the three rangemen sitting there, he did not believe this was that time.

But it was.

He finally leaned back, shoved out big oaken legs under the desk and said, 'I'll lock you up overnight for disturbin' the peace, and before daybreak I'll set you free—and you fellers go below town, then turn south-easterly. Nebraska's down there.' He allowed a moment to pass for protest to erupt. When none did erupt he heaved up to his feet, took down a ring of keys and pointed to his cell-room door.

A half-hour later when Ben had his prisoners locked up, the cell-room door barred again from his office-side, and he was rolling a smoke, Red Barton walked in. Ben finished making the smoke, nodded at Red, lit up and said, 'How's Walter?'

Red swung a chair and straddled it. 'Better'n Carl by a long shot. What did you do with them fellers, Ben?'

Albright used his smoking cigarette to point toward the cell-room door, then he said, 'How bad is Carl?'

'Busted nose, cracked ribs and a cracked jaw.' Red folded long arms around the back of the chair as he squatted there regarding Sheriff Albright. 'You goin' to charge 'em and keep 'em around until the circuit ridin' judge shows up?'

Albright had not come down in the last rain. He returned Red Barton's gaze as he said, 'Did Walt send you?'

Red cleared his throat. 'He's interested, Ben.'

'Yeah. He's got a right to be interested, hasn't he? . . . Hell, Red, why do you fellers always have to make a mountain out of a molehill?'

'I don't know what you mean, Ben.'

'Frank Tillitson told me over at the saloon one of you fellers rode into the yard over at

46

old Hatrack Hanson's place and shot a dog.'

'Well; the dog come at him. What else was he supposed to do?'

'The way it was told to me, Red, the dog didn't go after him. He just barked.' As he finished saying this and saw words forming on the red-headed man's lips, Sheriff Albright help up a big hand. 'All right; the dog ran at him. How about that squatter's milk cow last year up along Buffalo Creek—did she run at the feller who shot her?'

Red Barton sat in silence for a moment before saying, 'Ben, we got our interests to protect. You know that, for Chris' sake. If Walter looked the other way every time some son of a bitch came along and settled on land we been using for thirty years, we'd be squeezed out—and Mister Schultz is the biggest supporter of Hammersville's economy, don't forget that. What do emigrants contribute, tell me that, will you?'

Ben briefly recalled something like this the barman over at the saloon had said to him earlier in the day, and it was probably true. Ben Albright was no more knowledgeable about economics than Red Barton was, with the difference being that Red had had it drilled into him how important the Schultz cattle empire was to Brulé Valley, and all Ben Albright had ever felt was sympathy for cattle interests, *all* cattle interests.

He got things back where he could manage

them by saying, 'Did you figure that was a fair fight up on the roadway, Red?'

Barton nodded. He was Walt Schultz's rangeboss and one of the best stockmen in the territory. He was usually a fair-minded, honest man. 'Yeah, I'd say it was fair enough. Carl just lacked the heft. He could out-punch that cowboy, but in close he just didn't have the weight nor the power.'

Ben was already of an identical opinion. 'Then I don't figure to charge them,' he told Schultz's rangeboss.

'So you'll turn them out—when—in the morning?'

Ben stared across the desk at Barton. 'There is not goin' to be any more trouble, Red. Get that through your head. When you ride back to the ranch, you tell . . .'

Red's brown eyes were bright and hard. 'Go ahead, Ben, say the rest of it.'

Albright retreated. 'Just say I don't want any more made out of this. Walt will understand.'

Red smiled crookedly and leaned to push up to his feet. In a voice laced with sarcasm he said, 'Sure he'll understand.' Then the rangeboss walked out of the office into the night leaving Ben Albright with the beginning of a glimmer of forthcoming difficulties. Maybe balancing on the knife's edge was not going to be possible much longer.

He growled an earthy word into the silence, got to his feet and stamped out of the office on his way over to the café for three tins of stew and three more tins of black coffee.

His prisoners were not as hungry as they probably should have been. Being locked into jail cells had been in the backs of their minds since the episode up in northern Montana, and it was ironic that they were in cells now, six or seven hundred miles from northern Montana, for something altogether different; something they still felt thoroughly justified about. But they were still behind bars. As Cal drily said, 'If that lawman don't turn us loose in the morning, I'm goin' to have a bad feelin' about this business.'

Hugh was not worried. 'He'll turn us out. What's bothering me is that old bastard with the cane. You heard the talk over at the saloon. When that big old buzzard says jump everyone asks how high.'

Jack's hand was swollen. He slouched on his wall-bunk in the middle cell listening to his friends, and trying to keep the knuckles from becoming completely stiff by working them up and down. 'I wish I'd hit that damned fool with my left hand,' he plaintively said.

Hugh's dark eyes glinted smokily in recollection. 'You did all right with both hands ... But he knew how to fight, didn't he? I'd say he was maybe their best handfighter, which was why they let it go like that. Even old Schultz shut up after he got down there. They was sure he'd whip you.'

Jack was honest about that. 'Another thirty, forty pounds and he might have . . . You don't expect that damned lawman'll go up to the roominghouse and go through our saddlebags, do you?'

This thought may have come unexpectedly to Hugh and Cal because neither one of them commented for a while, then Cal blew out a big sigh and answered. 'If he does, we're goin' to have to lie like three Dutch uncles.'

For as long as this fearful prospect occupied their thoughts they were mostly silent, and later, when Sheriff Albright appeared in the dingy, poorly-lighted cellroom corridor, they watched him lean to shove a couple of little dented metal pails under each steel door, and waited. But when Ben stood up he simply said, 'Don't wait around town in the morning for the blacksmith to open up his shop. You can ride those worn-down shoes another four or five days, and by then you'll find another town.' He looked at Jack's swollen hand. 'You want some liniment?'

Jack went over to retrieve his pails of food as he answered. 'Naw. How's Carl?'

'Busted up a little.'

Jack already knew that. 'Too bad. He's one of those fellers who's pretty good at something, and who thinks he's *real* good at it. Sometimes they learn and sometimes they don't. He likely won't because he's young.' Jack stood inside holding his two pails and

50

looking through the steel straps at big Ben Albright. 'You figure that old son of a bitch is goin' to have someone out front in the morning, or maybe waiting down below town, don't you?'

Ben was candid about that. 'I said you was to get out of town before sunup. That's the reason. But I told his rangeboss there wasn't to be any follow-up.'

Hugh made a little sniffing sound. He remembered the expression on Schultz's face when Hugh had struck the older man with his own cane, then had contemptuously pitched aside the broken half. 'Sheriff, I got a feeling you never told Mister Schultz anything in your life . . . No, I'm not calling you a liar, I'm just sayin' that tellin' his rangeboss isn't the same as tellin' him—and my guess about Mister Schultz is that no one can tell him anything . . . They'll be out there.'

Cal entered the conversation with a pungent observation. 'I've seen his kind before in cattle country. We all have. If he don't own you, Sheriff, at least he's beyond your kind of law . . . You say anything to him or his rangeboss about Carl shootin' that dog up in the foothills? I'll bet you a new hat you didn't.'

Ben Albright's thick brows dropped a notch as he stared at Cal Hunter. 'Who told you about the damned dog?'

'We was in the saloon when Doctor Tillitson got mad at you over that. Remember?'

'Well; the darned dog made a run at Carl.'

Cal slowly wagged his head. 'No, he didn't make no run at him, Sheriff.' Cal had met that dog and he had neither offered to threaten Cal, nor had barked at him.

'How do you know?' demanded Ben Albright, and both Hugh and Jack turned slowly to gaze at their companion. Cal dared not say how he knew the dog was not vicious or he would arouse the lawman's suspicions about what the three of them had been doing up there above the foothills.

Cal bluffed his way through. 'Because I've rode into a hundred darned ranchyards and nearly every one of them had at least one dog, and I've yet to have one of them dogs really come after me.'

Ben Albright pointed. 'Eat your suppers. I'll see you before sunup in the morning.' He went up front, barred the cell-room door from the office side, blew down the lantern mantle, locked the jailhouse from out front and struck out for the lighted saloon upon the opposite side of the roadway, and northward. His mood was bad.

It was a week-night so there were only a few rangemen scattered among the drinkers and card-players at the saloon. Frank Tillitson was there and Sheriff Albright would have avoided the vinegary medical doctor if he could have but Ben was a large man; generally he was a head taller than any of the other customers.

Tillitson saw him and went along the bar to lean beside Albright. Frank had already downed a couple of jolts of popskull and was holding the third jolt in his skinny fist.

He said, 'If you want to talk to Schultz's cowboy about the light, I got him abed over at my cottage.' Frank downed his third jolt and put the sticky little glass atop the bar. 'Schultz fired him. Did you know that?'

Ben hadn't known it.

'You know why he fired him? Because he got whipped. He told me he'd send a man to town tomorrow with Carl's wages . . . You know, Ben, I was wrong about Walt Schultz. I told you I couldn't like him any more . . . I never should have tried to like him in the first place. He's an overbearing, big, sorry, bullying son of a bitch. Isn't he?'

The barman brought a bottle and glass, set them up in front of Sheriff Albright, exchanged a blank look with the lawman, then walked away. Doctor Tillitson eyed the bottle. 'You care to buy me a drink, Ben?'

Albright turned and looked down. 'No. You're smoked to the gills as it is, Frank.'

Tillitson accepted that. 'All right. Then you have one and we'll go down to the jailhouse so's I can look at that feller with the injured hand.'

Albright scowled.

Doctor Tillitson held up a bony finger and shook it. 'He's entitled to care and treatment.

That's the damned law, Ben . . . You want to buy me a drink and we can stand here and relax, or do you want to have one yourself, then accompany me down there?'

Ben filled the little sticky glass, filled his own glass, looked around the room as Doctor Tillitson tossed off his jolt, then looked down again. He had only seen Frank Tillitson drunk once before in all the years they had known each other. That had been about a year after Frank's wife had died. It had taken Frank that long to let the flood of tears come.

He was fond of Frank Tillitson—at times. Frank also irritated him, angered him, annoyed him, and at times upset him. But a man could like another man despite all these things, if the man was basically an honest individual, and Frank was honest. But he was also too outspoken, as with that remark he had made a short while ago about Walt Schultz—with two rangemen standing ten feet farther along the bar, gravely toying with their beer glasses and listening to every word Frank had said.

He took the medical man by the arm, took the bottle and both their glasses, and steered Frank to one of the distant, empty poker tables, then he sat him down and lit into him unmercifully for being drunk, for shooting off his mouth, and for being generally cantankerous. Frank sat slumped in his chair half-smiling, nodding his head at everything

54

the sheriff said to him, and mistily regarded the large, lurid painting above the back-bar of Custer's Last Stand.

CHAPTER SIX

A DARK NIGHT

The sheriff's word was good. It was still dark as the inside of a boot when he rattled his keys along the cell bars rousing all three prisoners. 'Get your boots on,' he ordered. 'It's time to go.'

They dressed. It took longest for Jack Brunner because he had to work with just one hand. His right hand was badly swollen and did not respond to mental commands.

Albright took them in darkness up to his office, gave them back their personal things, as well as their three shellbelts and holstered Colts. As he watched them buckle on the belts he drily said, 'Don't try to shoot me in the back, they aren't loaded.' Then he led them through his storeroom to the rear alley where their three horses were saddled and waiting.

Cal looked, squinted around at Ben Albright and said, 'Where are the bedrolls and saddlebags.'

The lawman answered indifferently. 'Wherever you left them. Get on those horses and start riding. And *keep* riding!'

Hugh swung up without a word. Jack hauled himself up too, and as Cal stepped across leather Hugh turned to ride up the alleyway. It was brighter outside than it had been inside the jailhouse, but it was still very dark. Before they reached the northerly intersecting roadway they could no longer see Sheriff Albright nor the alleyway out behind his jailhouse, and that pleased Hugh, who went unerringly in the direction of the roominghouse. There, they all piled off, looped their reins at the front fence and went inside. No one interrupted them as they got their saddlebags and bedrolls and returned to the roadway. From the saddle again Jack said, 'We better skirt along this side of town and leave some tracks like maybe we was actually heading southeasterly. Sure as hell old Schultz will send someone to look up our tracks.'

Neither Hugh nor Cal commented and when Jack led off his partners trailed along.

There was a slight chill in the air. Not enough of a chill to trouble men who had seldom ridden before dawn when it had not been cold though.

They went to the east end of Hammersville then down that side of the place; but out a hundred yards or so, and when they were nearing the lower end of the town where two roads diverged—one eastward, the other westward—Hugh suddenly reined to an abrupt halt and raised a warning hand to his companions.

What he had detected they all heard a moment later; walking horses coming down from the northeast. It sounded as though there might be four or five of them. Cal swore under his breath, then said, 'That damned sheriff—he did this on purpose.' As he finished speaking Cal hauled his horse around toward town.

They found a side-road and followed it soundlessly to the main thoroughfare a short distance north of the jailhouse. Cal glared in that direction, then struck out. They crossed to the west side of the slumbering town in single file. When they were again in the vicinity of the same alleyway they had left town by not fifteen minutes earlier, Cal kept riding westerly.

Upon the opposite side of town now, they halted again. This time they did not hear walking horses over across town; they heard what sounded like two more riders walking their horses down the main roadway—the same roadway they had crossed not five minutes earlier.

Jack gestured with his blue-wrapped right hand. 'Keep moving, Cal. Go towards the foothills. They got us cut off in the other directions. And be quiet.'

They rode sitting twisted in their saddles for a solid hour before Hugh straightened up and looked up ahead. He did not say he did not believe there was anyone behind them, he did not have to say it, his behaviour professed it adequately.

Cal was still angry. 'I'd like to go back and pot-shoot that damned lawman right where he sits down.'

Jack had been thinking about that. 'If he'd done that deliberately, why not just have those boys show up at the jailhouse and hand us over to them?'

Cal still grumbled.

They had been in the saddle a fair length of time when the cold seemed slightly more intense, and over in the east there was a hint of false-dawn. Hugh said, 'Open country. They can see us out here for ten miles.'

They loped for almost an hour, until they had the far foothills in sight as the light increased somewhat, and Jack shook his head. 'We're on our way back to the damned bear-cave.'

Hugh took the lead and angled in a different direction. He wanted at least to get a few of the foremost and lowest of those foothills at his back before sunrise occurred. He pushed his horse to do it, and when the sun finally appeared they had some of the lower, up-ended country behind them. And they halted up there to blow the horses and to climb a landswell and hunker up there, watching.

They did not see a single horseman. There were some cattle east of them only a couple of miles below the foothills, but that was all. Jack stood beside his horse after they came down

59

off the landswell and felt with his left-hand inside the saddlebags. Then he turned, smiling. 'Still there, underneath everything else.'

Cal immediately made his own search, but Hugh was still uncomfortable. Hills or no hills, what he wanted was some variety of close cover, such as trees. He reined off to his left before Cal had finished buckling down the saddle-bag flaps.

The sun climbed slowly, and just as slowly the cold diminished. They were riding abreast and talking a little, trying to satisfy themselves that Ben Albright had not really set them up for Walt Schultz's men to find, when Jack abruptly grunted and hauled back to a halt. Off on their left another rider was walking his horse up-country in their direction. The man had a shotgun in the crook of one arm. For several seconds, until they read all the signs correctly, all three of them thought the oncoming horseman was a manhunter. Then Hugh said, 'That's the old horse was in the corral down at that set of old buildings we saw from the forest. I don't know about the man, but I recognise that horse.'

The rider was slouching along watching underbrush. Evidently he was out early to pot-shoot some sagehens while they were out foraging for breakfast after being in a roost all night. He did not see the three rangemen sitting a short distance away watching him.

Then he did see them, because his dozing-along old horse suddenly threw up its head and halted stock-still. The separating distance was only about a hundred yards. The stranger was a tall, thin man with a shock of unruly brown hair. He did not look particularly young nor particularly old, but he certainly looked thin.

Jack raised his rein-hand in a salute, and that seemed to encourage the man on the old horse; he drummed on the horse's ribs to get the animal moving again, and rode up much closer.

He still did not look either young nor old, but he had a guileless smile as he dropped his rein-hand and ignored the shotgun to say, 'Good morning, gents. If you ride for Mister Schultz . . .'

Cal shook his head. 'If we was ridin' for anyone, friend, it wouldn't be Mister Schultz,' then, because he'd had a strong idea about this man's identity, he said, 'You live in that set of buildings up ahead a couple of miles or so?'

The lean man kept smiling as he nodded his head. 'Yes. My wife and I live there. She is the granddaughter of the man who proved up on that claim. His name was Hatrack Hanson. If you tellers been in the country long you've probably heard stories about him. Colourful old man.' The smile began to fade a little. 'My name is Leo Stanton.'

They nodded, and having satisfied most of the questions in their minds about Leo

61

Stanton, they relaxed in the saddle and Hugh said, 'You're the feller who got his dog shot.'

Leo Stanton regarded Hugh Cole over an interval of quiet before speaking again. 'How did you know that?'

Hugh almost smiled but not quite. Jack answered Stanton's question. 'We was in the saloon down in Hammersville when the sawbones down there told the sheriff about it. We overheard.' Jack paused, gravely considering the gawky-tall, thin man. 'By any chance did you know the cowboy who shot your dog?'

Leo Stanton shook his head. 'No. It happened too fast, and it was very early in the morning . . . And he rode out of the yard right afterwards.'

Hugh had a question for Leo Stanton. 'You live quite a distance from Hammersville. I'm curious about something: How did the doctor down there know your dog had been shot?'

'I told him. I rode down there in the night for medicine and all. He gave me everything he figured would help, and I came back home before sunup.'

Hugh looked down. 'On that old horse?' he asked, incredulously.

'No. On one of the horses I keep in the barn. Thoroughbred horses. I never put them out in the corrals. Would you like to see them? By now my wife'll have breakfast on the stove too.'

62

They gazed at the thin man. If ever a man appeared harmless, he did. He wasn't even carrying a belt-gun. Cal looked at his partners. 'I could sure eat,' he said.

They all could eat. Jack had one more question for the skinny man. 'You came out here and settled in to run cattle, Mister Stanton?'

'No. Horses. Fine quality horses. You'll see what I mean.' As he poked the old horse under him to life he smiled at the three rangemen. 'Thoroughbred horses, gents. There's never been a breed of horses like them. Not just for speed, but when they're bred-out right and handled right they'll make the finest cattle horses there ever was. Horses have always been my avocation.'

Hugh squinted over his shoulder. The land back there was empty. Even those cattle they had seen earlier to the eastward were no longer in sight. He straightened around and watched for those log buildings. But what troubled him now was not out-distancing any pursuit—as long as they kept moving—what troubled him was whether Walter Schultz had a man among his riders who could read sign. They had left tracks all the way up here from Hammersville, and even though the grass was strong and matted, if Schultz had one man who really understood sign, he would be back there somewhere like a hunting dog.

But they had a couple of hours' head start

63

so Hugh did not say anything as they came down beside a slip-rock landswell, rode around a bald, low pinnacle of an earthen hill, and had those old log buildings dead ahead in plain sight.

There was a wisp of white smoke arising from the back-room chimney, the old horse raised its head and nickered, and from inside the big old log barn there was an answering whinny or two. It was, taken all in all, a very pleasant, secluded and peaceful place.

A handsome, stocky woman came out onto the old porch carrying a Winchester rifle. The length of the barrel made her look smaller than she was. She did not smile, speak, nor move, she simply stood up there watching her husband ride in down at the barn accompanied by three men she had never seen before; but who looked to be hard, bronzed rangemen, the same kind of men who would ride with the man who had shot her dog.

Cal eyed the woman askance and so did Hugh. Jack spoke to Leo Stanton as he swung from the saddle. 'She won't commence shootin', will she?'

Stanton turned and sang out. 'Friends, Ellie—and I expect they're hungry.'

She did not go back inside for a few moments but eventually she did. Her husband turned a little apologetically. 'You got to understand, gents, she raised the dog from a sucklin' orphan. He was like a child to her.

From now any time a strange horseman come into the yard . . . well; she keeps that old Winchester rifle beside the door.'

Hugh had missed something back where they had first met. 'The dog's not dead yet?'

'No. As a matter of fact I guess the bullet didn't rip him open. When I got back with the medicines and all, Ellie had him washed up. I guess the bullet struck squarely beneath him and a sharp stone coming up from the ground ripped him open.' Leo Stanton stood a moment looking enquiringly at them. 'I should introduce you by name to my wife, gents.'

They told him their names, then followed him toward the house. The closer they got the sweeter was the aroma of pork gravy and biscuits and fresh, new coffee.

Cal was still trying to imagine what an 'avocation' was but he'd have allowed wild horses to drag him before he'd ever have asked.

CHAPTER SEVEN

THE STANTON PLACE

There was something about Ellie Stanton she might have inherited from her forebear, Hatrack Hanson. She had a tough, no-nonsense gleam in her eye, and even after she loosened a little toward the three strangers she was pouring biscuits and gravy and coffee into, she remained slightly reserved toward them.

She and her husband had come back to the old homestead from Chicago. Her husband had tuberculosis; they had told him in Illinois that unless he got out of the city to where there was clean air and better living conditions, he would die shortly.

He told them he had begun to feel much better after only a couple of months on the homestead. They listened politely and once or twice Hugh glanced over his shoulder out the window. The sun was climbing. Back down in Hammersville there would be some unhappy men, the foremost of which would probably be Walt Schultz.

Cal and Jack understood their partner's uneasiness and when they could not stow away another bite, they thanked Ellie Stanton as gallantly as they could, picked up their hats and started for the door. She side-tracked them. She had her injured dog in a wooden crate near the fireplace. They went dutifully over and looked at the animal. He was bandaged around the middle but his eyes were bright and he was alert. Jack said, 'He'll make it, ma'am,' and would have headed for the door but she pointed and said, 'Would you like me to make you a decent bandage for that hand, Mister Brunner?'

Jack looked down, the hand did not pain him as long as he did not try to use it, but it was discoloured now as well as being swollen. He said, 'Thanks, ma'm, but it's doing just fine,' and turned toward the door. He was the last one out. He turned, saw the handsome woman looking at him, and smiled before he closed the door.

Leo Stanton was a horseman, which surprised the men he led into the old log barn. City-men were ordinarily not as knowledgeable about animals as Leo Stanton proved himself to be.

He had three breedy mares in the barn and a magnificent stud-horse—what people in the east called a stallion. Even Hugh forgot his urge to ride on, for a short while, and during that time Stanton led each animal out, showed them to best advantage, spoke of their bloodlines, pointed out both their strong and weak points, and put them back into their stalls.

Cal, Jack and Hugh were impressed. Like

all rangeriders, they were familiar with horses as a tool of their trade, and also because they liked animals, but a cowboy was rarely a horseman. There was an adage about that: A cowboy was a man who knew a little about cattle and usually knew a damned sight less about horses.

Finally, Hugh looked out back, judged the time from the sun's position, and herded his partners out where their dozing horses were waiting, and from over along the porch of the main-house Ellie called out.

'Riders coming, Leo . . . I don't like the looks of them. It might be Schultz's men again.'

Jack, in the act of untying his horse to mount, stepped clear for a hard look in all directions. He did not see any riders. Leo Stanton pointed. 'From the front of the house you can see down past some wide hills to the open range.' He dropped his arm. 'If it's Schultz's men you hadn't better be in the yard when they get here.'

That was probably true, but it also rankled. Hugh was turning his horse to mount when Stanton said that. He stopped, gazing back at the horse-rancher.

Jack held up a hand. They could all hear loping horses now. Stanton gestured again with an upraised skinny arm. 'They'll come around that hill in a minute or two.'

Cal swore, then growled at his companions.

'Get the horses in the barn. We couldn't get clear now, anyway.'

Whether it was a good suggestion or not, that is what they did, and while they were turning their animals into empty stalls Leo Stanton was standing there, looking a little perplexedly at them. For the first time since meeting the three rangemen, it was beginning to dawn on him that they were not just the transient cowboys he had assumed that they were. Not after the way they hurried inside the barn after one of them had said they couldn't get away now anyway. He was still standing in a puzzled way when Cal came out of the stall he had put his horse in, and in plain sight yanked free the tie-down on his holstered Colt.

Hugh and Jack did the same thing. For Jack, handling the sixgun was a little awkward because he had to use his left hand. But it was Jack Brunner who cleared up the bafflement for Leo Stanton. By now they could all hear the riders coming toward the yard.

Jack said, 'Leo, tell them anything you want to tell them, but keep them out of this barn. And you haven't seen three men. You understand?'

Stanton understood. He also remembered something else. The one called Cal had told him at their first meeting that Mister Schultz would be the last man they would ride for, or something about like that. With the approaching horsemen drawing steadily closer

69

he said, 'By any chance did you fellers have trouble with Mister Schultz or his riders?'

Jack gestured with his blue-bandaged hand. 'We can talk later. Get out there and do what you got to do, but keep them out of here. *Go on!*'

Leo went. Cal, Hugh and Jack faded into the perpetual gloom of the old log barn's interior. Jack went to the doorless big square rear opening and looked out. There was nothing to be seen to the north, south or west from that position, but he had not expected to see much.

Cal was on the south side of the barn where some rotting, ancient harness was draped over a saddle-pole. He could see the oncoming riders. There were three of them, not five as Cal had expected. They rode into the yard at a walk and each man had a carbine buckled into position beneath his fender. That impressed Cal because ordinarily rangeriders did not carry carbines if they were working. If they were hunting—men or anything else—they would carry them.

Hugh hissed and pointed directly toward the approaching horsemen. Cal leaned for a better look, and recognised the man with the red hair.

Stanton was leaning on his tie-rack out front, and to his credit, whether or not he was quaking inside, he leaned there looking as relaxed and calm as a man could be. When the

70

rangemen stopped a couple of yards away and Red Barton spoke to Stanton, every word carried to the listening three men inside the barn.

Barton said, ' 'Morning. We're lookin' for some fellers who might have come up through here.'

Leo played his part perfectly. 'What fellers? What did they look like?'

Red Barton described Cal, Jack, and Hugh while the pair of men with him sat gazing elsewhere, hands atop saddlehorns, completely at ease. One of them was a hawk-faced, rawboned man with straight black hair and dark eyes. While Leo was listening to Barton, this hawk-faced man gradually finished studying all the buildings, and dropped his head to look at the dusty yard. Hugh was watching this man more closely than either of the other two. He had already guessed why Barton was here—someone had led him here, probably by horse-sign. Hugh eased out his sixgun and let it dangle at his side.

Leo was shaking his head when he said, 'If they were around, I didn't see them. But then I was out hunting sagehens earlier and they could have passed through.'

Barton's brown gaze went over to the main-house. 'Maybe your wife saw 'em,' he said, and Leo, having anticipated that, had a rebuttal handy.

'If she did she'd have told me when I came

71

back. And why would any riders who were being chased come here anyway? Not into the yard, not to kill time with me and my wife if they knew you were after them.'

Red said, 'Yeah. Well; maybe they didn't figure anyone was down their back trail.'

Leo shot a question at Barton. 'What did they do? Aren't you Walter Schultz's rangeboss? Did they do something to Mister Schultz?'

Red gazed at the skinny man for a while before replying. 'Yeah, I'm the rangeboss. We've never met. My name is Red Barton and I already know your name.'

Leo nodded about that and repeated his question. 'What did they do, Mister Barton?'

Again, Red Barton deliberated before speaking. 'They broke out of jail,' he said, and would have said more but Leo Stanton did not allow him the opportunity.

'If they broke out of jail, why isn't Sheriff Albright here with you?'

The men in the barn, with a good head-on view of Barton, saw the annoyance beginning to show when Barton answered. 'They tried to clean out the town yesterday, and one of our riders got hurt.'

Stanton said something that proved he was either tactless or unaware of the risks. 'One of your men shot our dog, Mister Barton. I guess I couldn't sympathise with your rider that was hurt.' Then he shifted position slightly on the tie-rack and, looking steadily up into the face of the rangeboss, added more. 'No one rode through here that I know of. But if you were the sheriff instead of Mister Schultz's foreman, I'd feel better about you riding over my land trying to make trouble for people.'

Hugh started to raise his fist with the sixgun in it. So did Jack, but Cal, with the best view of them all, did not move. The hawk-faced rangerider turned abruptly toward Red Barton and said, 'Let's get back. This ain't goin' to do no good.'

The other cowboy was stonily regarding Leo. Neither he nor Barton seemed to have heard the hawk-faced man, so he growled more insistently at them. 'We're wasting time, there ain't no one here and we still got a lot of country to cover. Come along, Red.'

Barton finally lifted his rein-hand, but the expression on his face was almost fierce. He turned once for a final stare, then eased his horse around.

They left the yard behind the hawk-faced man, riding westward. Hugh stepped to the rear barn opening to watch while Cal and Jack remained up front waiting for Leo Stanton to enter the barn.

The skinny man walked into the barn, went to the saddle-pole and leaned there a moment as though he would collapse, then he looked Cal squarely in the eye and said, 'Who are you men? What did you do down in

73

Hammersville?'

Cal's answer was laconic. 'We told you our names, friend; that's exactly who we are. What we done down in Hammersville is about like Barton said. We got into a squabble with him and some other fellers, and that's how Jack's hand got hurt—he walloped the whey out of the one that shot your dog, the feller named Carl.'

Stanton scowled. 'How do you know he's the one who shot my wife's dog?'

'It came out,' replied Cal Hunter, 'along with a lot of other stuff.'

Hugh walked up toward the front of the barn looking worried. He ignored Stanton to address his partners. 'That black-haired feller with the hawk-nose . . . sure as I'm standing here he tracked us. I thought he was actin' odd out there.'

Stanton said, 'He didn't see you or they'd have—'

'He didn't have to see us,' stated Hugh Cole. 'He was looking at the ground while you and Barton was talking. I watched him. He was reading the sign where we rode in, and where we walked over to the mainhouse, and walked back down here. Sure as hell he knew we were in this barn. That's why he kept tryin' to get Barton away from the front opening. If there was a fight he knew damned well who was going to get shot.' Hugh gestured. 'They rode west. There aren't goin' to be any fresh tracks

74

out there. He'll lead 'em in a big surround, and they're not goin' to find any tracks out there either.' Hugh dropped his arm and gazed steadily at Jack Brunner. Jack gravely nodded his head.

'If we left no tracks out yonder, then that means we're still here, don't it?' he said.

Hugh did not reply, he instead turned to go once more to the back of the barn where he could still see those three horsemen.

Cal finally spoke. 'All right. Let 'em ride west. We'll ride east.'

Jack had been standing there, thumbs hooked, staring at the sunbright yard out front, deep in thought. When Cal spoke Jack turned slightly. 'What about Stanton?' he asked Cal Hunter. 'By now they know he lied to them.' Jack jerked one thumb loose of the belt and used it to indicate the building they were standing in. 'It'll burn like straw, Cal. This time of year these old log buildings will go up like a damned torch.'

Cal needed no further elaboration. There was one completely efficient tool range-cattlemen had been using against settlers since the very first range war: Fire. Rarely were incendiarists caught, and when their buildings, all their possessions and sometimes their animals or children were burned to death, homesteaders lost the will to resist.

During the silence which followed what he had said, Jack looked down where Hugh was standing, then back again. 'Schultz would do it, Cal.'

There was no need to affirm this. Cal knew perfectly well that Walter Schultz would do it. He might even have wondered why Schultz had not had it done before, if Hugh had not come striding back to say, 'They're turning north, farther into the foothills. I'd guess they'll turn east eventually too, and they damned well might find our tracks where we came down from the bear-cave. That ground was still soft when we rode over it.'

The implication to this was not lost on either Hunter nor Brunner, although Leo Stanton leaned there staring from man to man not quite grasping the significance. Then Hugh spoke again and Stanton fixed his attention upon Cole.

'We can head south, keep the buildings between us and them as long as possible, then run for it. We can get clear that way.'

Jack jerked his thumb in Stanton's direction. 'They'll sure as hell burn him out, Hugh, and maybe do worse if his wife is in the house at night when they come back to do it.'

Cole rolled this around in his mind for a while then faced Jack. 'All right. Then maybe *we* better do some manhunting.'

It had been an ambiguous thing to say but Hugh's partners understood it, whether the skinny horserancher did or not. Then Hugh added a little more because it was on a topic

76

which had been uppermost in all their minds for a long time now.

'And if we ever see Mexico it'll be a damned miracle.'

CHAPTER EIGHT

THE AMBUSH

They had the surrounding foothills to help them get away from the ranch, but even so, as Jack suggested, if Red Barton or that hawk-faced man with him were *coyote*, they wouldn't just go dogging it up and around reading tracks or hunting for them, they would also climb atop some of the low, fat hills and sit up there until they saw movement.

But Hugh expected Barton to do this, and accordingly went a considerable distance out of their way to manage always to have some foothills around them.

This did not mean they could not be located by movement, but it *did* mean it would be harder to locate them, and even harder to identify them.

They did not have a plan, just a goal. They had no idea what would happen if they were fortunate enough to ambush Schultz's rangemen; but they were shrewd, wily men and whether they were correct or not in their aggressive belief that if they could neutralise Schultz's manhunters they would be able to get southward without immediate danger, they were now fully embarked upon attempting to effect that ambush.

The heat was rising, finally, but there was a high, diaphanous mistiness across the sky, as though there might be rain on the way, and this diffused the heat to some extent, making it rather pleasant riding weather. And Hugh was careful. He acted as though the success of their venture depended entirely upon him, but that was Hugh Cole's nature; he wanted to excel.

They lost sight of the log buildings before they had been an hour in the saddle, and if they had not known those buildings were back there, they would have thought they were passing through an utterly uninhabited countryside, exactly as they had thought when they had been up at the bear-cave before they saw the log buildings.

There was cattle sign, which there had not been before, and Cal guessed that perhaps Barton and his companions had brought over a band with them on their way to the Stanton place. Whether this was so or not, when they finally saw a few head in among the broken low hills, they had a large Circle S on their right ribs.

Twice, Hugh sashayed until he could pick up Barton's sign. He followed it for a mile each time, then abandoned it in favour of protective cover. All he had wanted to ascertain was Barton's course and direction. When they did that the last time Hugh squinted for the location of the sun, decided

79

that Barton would be about ready to head for the home-ranch in order not to arrive there in the dark, and swung his arm to indicate the route he thought they should take to make an interception. Cal and Jack were perfectly agreeable. They had been satisfied to leave it up to Hugh Cole.

They halted in mid-afternoon at a cold-water spring where the horses filled up, where the men also drank, and where Jack soaked his swollen hand. The discolouration was unabated but Jack thought some of the swelling had departed. He worked his fingers a little to test this idea, and smiled. The fingers worked well and did not pain him.

From this point they dropped southward almost to the last break in the land, and had a sweeping view of Brulé Valley southward and eastward. It was Cal who caught movement from the side of his eye and raised an arm to point.

There were three horsemen slouching along down a long slot of the foothills evidently on their way to the open country below, and they were riding as men did who were bored or discouraged, or maybe both, as well as hungry.

Hugh made his judgment of the distance, and led off around a wide, low hill. They loped for a while, then dropped back to a steady walk. Where Hugh wanted to intercept Barton and his two companions was at the edge of the open range. He would have preferred to make the interception back in among the foothills but that would be impossible; Hugh and his partners had to cross too much country, and Barton with his companions was not riding fast, but the distance he had to cover to reach open country was not very great. In fact, as Cal and Jack saw, if Hugh misjudged either the distance, or the time they had to cross it in, Barton and his riders would be out of the foothills—and going after them in open country would be more than simply dangerous, it could be deadly.

Hugh took a risk; he led off in another lope for a quarter of a mile, then faded behind a landswell and rode at a steady walk with Barton and his friends upon the far side of the same landswell. All three men palmed their sixguns. Where the landswell petered out, diminishing until it met and became part of the southward wide flow of open range, would be about where the meeting would occur.

Jack leaned and said, 'Hugh; just one of us ought to show himself where the slope drops down. They'll turn toward him sure as hell.'

Cole thought about that, then shrugged as though he could live with the suggestion but was not enthusiastic about it. 'You two hang back,' he said, and urged his horse on into a faster walk.

Cal and Jack looked for shelter. There was none. Not close enough to be of any help to them. Jack, with his suggestion being turned into action, had to come up with something, and squinted along the upper flat rim of the landswell. It was not a very good idea, but he jerked his head at Cal and began working his way up along the sidehill toward the topout. When they edged up there, halting just below the rim, they could see Schultz's riders very clearly; clear enough in fact to make out Barton's red hair.

They could also see Hugh. He was less than fifty yards from the tapering area where the landswell sank toward the onward flat country. Cal swung off, pulled out his carbine, sank to one knee and waited. Jack remained in the saddle. A carbine was useless to a one-handed man.

He could see Barton though, and when he and his two companions were about to appear upon the far side of the landswell, Jack called softly to Cal. 'Let's go down the far side and be behind those bastards.' Instead of waiting to see whether Cal would comply, Jack reined up over the topout and rode down the far slope in plain sight.

Cal came over behind him, with his carbine being balanced by one hand across his lap.

Barton's men saw Hugh, and yanked back to a startled stop. Hugh immediately whirled and started back the way he had come. He looked up along the landswell, was still looking up there for sign of Jack and Cal, when someone back down-country let fly with a sixgun shot.

The range was too great, but Hugh had no doubt but that the pursuing rangemen would now resort to their Winchesters.

He saw where his partners had gone over the landswell and hauled his horse around to do the same thing. Behind him the spurring rangemen were in full pursuit, and because Walt Schultz was one of those cowmen who believed that good horses were essential to a successful cattle operation, his riders were well mounted. They were beginning to close the gap when Hugh was nearing the topout. Hugh sank down the off side of his horse, was momentarily silhouetted against that milky sky, and as two carbines were fired upward in his direction, his horse lowered its head and plunged ahead down the far side out of Barton's sight.

Mid-way down the slope Jack and Cal were beside their fidgeting horses, guns ready. They scarcely heeded Hugh. They were waiting for Barton to come charging over the topout too.

He and his companions did exactly that. Hugh was unable to draw his saddlegun, there had not been sufficient time, so he stood wide-legged in front of his horse and fired into the dirt in front of the three oncoming horsemen, who were no longer brandishing their guns, but were desperately seeking to check their plunging horses.

At the last possible moment they had suddenly become aware of the possibility of an ambush—but their horses hadn't. Barton and the hawk-faced men were carried over the topout and down the slope directly toward the three dismounted men who were bleakly waiting. The third cowboy fought his horse around and sank in the spurs. The horse sprang back and gave a big bound heading down the way he had recently lunged upwards. In seconds that man was lost to view, but Barton, less than three hundred feet from three men aiming guns at him, yelled out.

'Hold it! Don't shoot!'

The hawk-faced man took his cue from the rangeboss and held up both arms as far as his rein-hand would allow him to. He was signifying that he too was no longer willing to fight.

Barton got his excited horse under control, just barely, and alternately looked at the three stationary gunmen aiming weapons at him, and his excited mount. The hawk-faced man had a more quiet animal. When he yanked it back to a halt the horse did not move again. The hawk-faced man still had both arms raised. He was staring at the men on the ground in front.

Cal called roughly to Red Barton. 'Get down, you son of a bitch, and drop that carbine! You too, hooknose—get down and let go that damned gun!'

Barton and the other man obeyed. Barton's horse finally began to turn less agitated now that there was no one on his back.

Jack Brunner turned, mounted his animal and rode up the slope. Near the topout he swung off and went upwards until only his head showed. Near the bottom of the landswell there was a writhing man on the ground, hatless and clearly in great pain. Southward was his riderless horse, running belly down with the reins and stirrups flapping. Jack mounted, kept his cocked sixgun in his left hand, and rode down there.

The writhing cowboy looked up from an ashen face, saw the gun and recognised the burly man holding it, and said, 'Leg's busted. The damned horse stumbled and fell an' rolled on my left leg.'

Jack neither changed expression nor spoke. He swung off, walked ahead, yanked loose the cowboy's Colt and flung it away, then put up his own gun and said, 'Stop wriggling!' The cowboy tried to obey but the pain was bad. He still writhed a little and had his jaws locked so hard the muscles stood out. Jack ignored these things as he knelt and reached for the broken leg, felt along the trouser until he found the break, then gripped both the upper leg and lower leg, and without glancing at the man's face, gave a powerful jerk in opposite directions.

The cowboy fainted.

Jack finally looked at the man's face. All that exertion had started Jack's injured right hand hurting again. He slit the man's trousers then got up to forage for something to fashion a splint out of, and had to settle for two old dry twigs which were crooked and as hard as rock.

He went to work impassively, using strips of the cowboy's torn trousers to make the binding. He was finishing up when four horsemen came back across the topout at a walk and started down toward him. He looked up at them, was satisfied with what he saw, then resumed his work. There was no waste motion and no indecisiveness. He had done this before; most rangemen had, who had been at their trade any number of years.

When Hugh and Cal rode up with their silent, disarmed captives, Cal leaned and said, 'What you got, Jack?'

The answer was gruffly given. 'A damned fool that falls off'n horses.'

'Where's the horse?'

'Gone,' stated Jack curtly, rising to dust off his knees and look at the unconscious man. 'Damned horse is probably half way home by now.' He stonily stared downward. 'Now what are we goin' to do? He can't walk and I wouldn't let the son of a bitch use my horse if he was the Angel Gabriel.' Jack lifted baleful eyes to Red Barton and the hawk-faced man. 'Get down,' he growled. 'Hoist him up between you and start walking!'

Barton looked from the unconscious man to Jack Brunner. He had good reason to respect

Jack Brunner. He had seen what Brunner could do when he was angry. But as Barton stepped down he said, 'It's too far. It's at least twelve miles to town.'

Hugh and Cal swung to the ground and stood, reins dangling from their fingers. Hugh looked coldly at Red Barton. 'If you'd caught us, and one of us was lyin' there with a busted leg, what would you do?'

'He'd make us carry him like we're goin' to make him do,' stated Cal.

Hugh and the hawk-faced man looked at one another. The hawk-faced man said, 'What's your name?'

Hugh's reply was slow coming. 'What the hell business is it of yours?'

'I'm a 'breed too,' said the hawk-faced man. 'My name is Harold White.'

Hugh showed no empathy. 'You ride for Schultz—you're a bastard,' he replied, and pointed out where the injured man's gun was lying in the buffalo grass. 'Pick it up!'

Red Barton said, 'Don't move, Harold.'

The hawk-faced man did not move, except to turn his eyes away from Hugh Cole.

CHAPTER NINE

ESCAPEES

Surprisingly, it was Jack Brunner who, in a palaver with his partners, finally said, 'All right. It's a sight close to the Stanton place.'

Hugh and Cal accepted that but Hugh had something to add to it. 'We got Schultz's rangeboss along with the other two. When they don't show up—and when that loose horse comes home . . .'

Cal scowled. 'Well; what do you want to do, turn 'em loose?'

Hugh glanced over where the hawk-faced man named Harold White was down on one knee beside the injured man. Red Barton was also considering the injured man, but standing up as he did so. Hugh said, 'I guess so, Cal. Let Barton pack his friend with the busted leg behind the cantle.' He looked around at both Cal and Jack. 'If we take 'em to the Stantons— then what? Schultz will find them over there, sure as hell, and if Stanton had trouble before it won't hold a candle to what he'll have then. He'll think they helped us. And Stanton's a fine horseman—I guess—but all I've ever seen him hold onto is a shotgun.'

Jack made a rueful little smile. 'His wife'd give old Schultz all the fight he'd want.'

Hugh ignored that. 'We got to decide.'

Jack did not particularly want Barton and the other two men to go back to their home-place. That would certainly ensure real trouble. But they had real trouble on their hands anyway. He finally said, 'All right; let 'em go—and we turn south. It'll be dark by the time we pass Hammersville. If we get down that far I guess they won't find us.'

Cal turned to call over to Red Barton. 'Boost that friend of yours onto a horse. The three of you get going. Forget the guns, and don't even look back.'

Barton studied the three partners as though he might have something to say. Harold White growled something and Barton turned to look down. He and Harold White got the chalky-faced rider onto his one good leg. They brought their horses over. The injured man's lips were nearly bloodless when his companions boosted him astride, then mounted with him. As they reined past, down the west side of the barren landswell, Barton put a cold, hostile look downward but did not say a word.

After Schultz's cowboys were down-country beyond the landswell, angling easterly, Jack went after his mount. He swung up, waited until his partners were also astride, then said 'Southeastward?'

Hugh Cole nodded. That, he thought was the general direction of Arizona, but even if he

89

was off in his guesswork they could correct their course because they had hundreds of miles to cover.

It was hot out upon the open range, but the air had a faintly sultry feel to it. Cal studied the milky sky a long while then offered his opinion.

'It's goin' to ball up and rain again. Maybe someone Up There is favourin' us like He did the last time it rained. Won't be any tracks.'

Jack was massaging his sore hand and said nothing. Hugh was riding in contemplation of something neither of his partners had a part in. Being a 'breed had its drawbacks. Not on the open range nor in cattle camps, but in the cities and towns it did. Still, when a man was neither fish nor fowl, he had no choice but to make the best of it. As for other 'breeds, such as that man back in the foothills with Schultz's rangeboss, probably because when it came right down to it, what mattered was whether a man was a *man* was what actually mattered; there was not any kinship—except between partners. He looked at Cal, squinting into the waning day, and Jack, resting his sore hand atop the saddlehorn as he slouched along, grunted to himself and also turned to study the onward flow of country.

They did not halt until some trees in the distance got close enough so that their animals could detect the scent of water. Then they rode on over there, found the creek, saw a mile-long, massive blackberry thicket, swung off to tank up the animals and rest a while, hunt for ripe blackberries and fill up on them.

Jack bathed his sore hand in the cold water. He hunkered there for fifteen minutes, until all the pain was gone and he had used both paws to sluice off with, then he went over where Hugh was resting with his hat over his face and said, 'In a way I sort of dislike the idea of tuckin' tail.'

The voice from beneath the hat sounded as though it came from a deep well. 'You don't look like Sir Galahad to me.'

Jack hunkered down. 'Who?'

For a moment no sound came from beneath the hat, and when it did it was to ask a question. 'You see any riders out there?'

Jack looked. Visibility was diminishing but it was still good enough to see a fair distance. 'No,' he replied, and went back to his earlier thoughts. 'One more good lick and we'd have busted that old son of a bitch down to size.'

Cal strolled up with his hat one-third full of ripe blackberries. He sat down as Hugh spoke again from beneath the hat. 'The first time they didn't know us. The second time, we got lucky. Partner, Walter Schultz is the kind that rolls up over you with all the riders and guns he can hire, and I guess he's rich enough to hire quite a crew.' Hugh lifted his hat. 'You goin' to eat all those berries, Cal?'

Hunter leaned to put the hat down. 'Help

yourself—but my maw used to say if a person ate too many of them things he'd get the green-apple quickstep.'

Hugh sat up, scratched his head, then scooped up a handful of berries, popped them one at a time into his mouth and gazed back the way they had come. He finally said, 'We're safe. He can't find us in the dark and tomorrow we'll be even farther away.' Then he smiled at Jack Brunner. 'He'll be frothin' at the mouth.'

Brunner eased down in the soft creek-side grass, watched their horses for a while, then fished around for his makings. As he worked up a hump-backed cigarette because his right hand was not up to this kind of fine work yet, he said, 'I got an uncomfortable feelin' old Schultz won't take this settin' down. I don't think he'd take the other things settin' down either.'

Cal wiped off berry juice. 'What can he do if he can't catch up to us?'

Jack was not prepared to answer that so he said, 'I'll feel better in a few days when we're plumb out of this country,' then he too scooped up a handful of berries.

They left the creek shortly before dusk, still holding to a southwesterly course, and they rode without haste. Jack's hand felt much better; and when he held it up close, he could determine that despite his most recent exertions when he had set that cowboy's leg, quite a bit of the swelling had departed.

Cal said, 'Two, three more days, and you'll be as good as new.'

They rode for a steady five hours over country they could not have described once nightfall arrived, then went down into a wide, shallow place where there was a creek, and washed the backs of their animals, draped saddleblankets sweat-side up, and unrolled their bedding. Cal was kicking out of his boots when he said, 'I could eat the tail end out of a mountain lion if someone would hold its head.'

Jack nodded. He was also hungry. 'How the hell did In'ians go for days livin' on stuff like blackberries, Hugh?'

Cole was unbuckling his gunbelt when he said, 'Did they?'

Jack looked around. 'Didn't they? I used to hear stories like that when I was a kid. How they'd trot on foot for days on end eatin' grass seed, berries, stuff like that.'

Hugh rolled up his shellbelt, placed it within six inches of where his head would be when he crawled into the blankets, and said, 'I'm a steak and potato man, Jack. Berries are fine, when you can't get anything else.' He yawned. 'The only thing I can tell is something my mother told me one time, when I was a kid— when the Indians was rounded up and reservationed and the gover'ment sent in a big herd of cattle for 'em to shoot an' eat, about half of 'em couldn't stand the smell when they

93

roasted cow-meat, and the other half threw up after eating it. They were used to wild game; it tastes a lot different. You know that as well as I do . . . Good night.'

Cal got up three times during the night. He had eaten the most blackberries, and his mother had been right. Some men live and learn, and some men just live.

They left the swale-camp about sunrise, the horses were fresh, the day was not going to be as warm as the previous days had been, that veiled mistiness had firmed up during the night and now there was a very noticeable high overcast. Hugh thought they might cover enough ground over the next few days to be out of range by the time the rain came, but Cal shook his head. That was all they had to occupy themselves with as they rode away the morning, except when they came over a low, wide roll of grassland and started up a big band of pronghorns. They were beyond handgun range, and by the time they swung off with carbines, the antelope were an additional mile distant.

There was not an animal around that could out-run an antelope; the fleetest thoroughbred horse could not stay within gunrange unless he was within gunrange when he came onto the little critters, and then he could only hold that parity for a minute or two.

They mounted up, watched the distant dust, and Cal groaned.

The heat was less but because of increasing sultriness it seemed undiminished. Still, there was no direct sunlight; it was diffused by that miles-wide accumulating overcast.

They were mid-way into the afternoon when a mountain pass appeared directly ahead. They speculated that there would probably be a road up through there. Any pass with the low and gradual incline of this particular pass, usually had been used by drovers or travellers with wagons, even if it was not still being used.

But they did not get close to the pass until near the end of the day. It was one of those phenomena that occurred often in clear-air country; riders could head for a mountain pass which seemed to be no more than perhaps four or five miles ahead, and although they rode for a solid two hours towards it, they never seemed to get much closer.

Finally, though, when they could discern individual trees up there, and banks of stone and shale, the same thought occurred to all three of them.

The east-west stageroad out of Hammersville went down below town before bearing *away* in those two different directions. For miles there was no hindrance, the land was more or less flat, but eventually there was the inevitable need to get through the mountains which made Brulé Valley a big punchbowl, and by the time Hugh, Cal and Jack were close enough to smell resin and hear birds in the pine and fir trees, they could also make out a strip of road going up through that low and gradual pass, which was still being used, and obviously very often. There was dust in the ruts, not even the more rugged weeds grew where steel tyres passed along, and Jack Brunner leaned on his saddleswells squinting up the gloomy pass.

'What d'you know,' he mildly said, 'we rode half the darned length of the valley from Hammersville over grassland when we could have found a decent roadbed to ride over.'

That of course was the price they had paid for not being familiar with the territory. Not that it made all that much difference.

Jack led off up into the trees, leaving the open range behind. It was cooler up there and the scent was different. It also got darker the farther they went.

From each side of the road where the foremost stands of timber were, it appeared there would be nothing but more timber to the north and south, but when they dipped down into a little swale where a creek crossed the road over a bed of round stones, it was possible to discern a park on their left through the trees. Jack turned toward it without a word. It was time to make camp.

They might have found another, bigger and perhaps even better park up ahead somewhere, but they were savvy rangemen; they never tempted fate when they had

96

something satisfactory at hand.

There was water, they could hear it out through the trees, but it did not enter their glade. They unsaddled and led the animals through the settling gloom, searching. When they finally found the watercourse, it was the horses which had led the men to it, not the other way around.

This time, when they unrolled their blankets each man placed his naked Winchester beside the coiled gunbelt and Colt. There was a wide variety of predators who lived in primitive timber country, and if they could pick up the smell of horses—and the horses were hobbled—whether they got a meal off the horses or not, they could certainly kill them.

Cal said, 'Speakin' as a rich man, I can say that right here an' now I'd give ten dollars for a fifty cent beefsteak with spuds and gravy.'

Jack had the customary flat tins of sardines in his saddlebags. For that matter so did Cal as well as Hugh. Jack opened his tin, ate with a stick, drank the oil and made a loud belch before saying, 'You better quit squanderin' your wealth, Cal. Before you know it you'll be back to cowboying for a living.'

They watched the horses for a while. Jack made a wide scout of the area, brushing trees and scrub-brush here and there, then returned to camp. He had not gone out looking for bears or cougars to frighten off, he had gone out to define the area where he and his friends were camping by leaving man-scent. Usually, that was all it took.

They crawled in and Hugh heaved a big sigh, then spoke. 'Old Schultz will be tied in knots by now. I wonder if anyone ever made him look like a horse's ass before and got away with it?'

No one replied, but it was unlikely that anyone had.

'Every time he shows his ugly face in Hammersville folks're goin' to snicker behind their hands. Three saddletramps came out of nowhere, made him an' his outfit eat crow, then rode on again.'

Cal pointedly said, 'Good night!'

Hugh said no more, but for a while he lay back gazing up at the misty, high overcast sky, wearing a satisfied expression.

CHAPTER TEN

SURPRISE!

The thing which awakened Jack Brunner was a slight pressure, the kind men who slept on the ground occasionally encountered even after they had brushed the ground where they had tossed their bedrolls. Only this time it was not a small round rock, although Jack drowsily thought it was and felt back gropingly to push it away.

It was a gunbarrel. The cold steel was unmistakable. Jack opened his eyes, pulled his hand back, and very slowly turned his head. The man hunkering there looking at him was bearded, dark, had a muffler around his throat and a dirty old brown hat tipped forward. He was a stranger. As he and the man with the gun exchanged a long look, Jack became gradually conscious of the highwaymen who probably made a living up through these mountains, particularly along the tree-lined stagecoach road. His second thought was of the fortune at the bottom of his saddlebags, then the stranger softly said, 'Lie still, mister,' and leaned slightly to flick Jack's emptied holster. Evidently the stranger had been there for some little time.

Jack stopped moving. Behind him a couple

99

of yards he heard someone quietly but gruffly say, 'Lie back or I'll split your skull!'

Jack made no attempt to look over there. He let his breath out slowly, and listened. There obviously was more than just one man.

Then he heard a voice he recognised. 'Sit up. Don't do anything silly, just sit up.'

There were three of them and one of them was that sheriff named Ben Albright from Hammersville. Jack swung his eyes to the bearded man. There was nothing to be read from the bearded man's face but wariness and resolution.

The sheriff finally raised his voice, sounding relieved as he said, 'All right, gents, on your feet. Never mind the holsters, we already got your weapons. Pull your boots on, we got a hell of a ride ahead of us.'

Jack eyed his bearded captor. The man nodded without speaking and Jack got out of his bedroll, felt for his boots, cast a sidelong glance where his weapons had been, found both the holster and the saddlegun scabbard empty, and concentrated on getting ready to stand up.

For once, Cal Hunter said nothing, and Hugh, who would not have said anything, anyway, was the first one to stand up and glance around.

How the sheriff and his two possemen had covered all that distance in such a short space of time—he could not possibly have known

100

where Jack, Cal and Hugh had been, before that man with the broken leg had returned to Schultz's home place, and someone then had had to ride into town—kept Jack and his partners silent and baffled until Ben Albright's men went after the horses. During their absence the sheriff was expansive. It was late, it was cold, he loathed doing this kind of possework, but he had managed to bring it off, and that fairly well made up for all the rest of it. Nor was Ben Albright mean or vindictive by nature. He holstered his Colt, plunged both hands into coat pockets and recognised the expressions on the unshaven faces in front of him as he said, 'You boys had ought to know a country better, before you get into trouble. There's three cow camps south of the road about ten miles apart.' He waited for someone to understand the implication and when no one did, perhaps because his prisoners were still a little sleep-drugged, he said, 'Relays. We changed horses three times.'

Cal accepted that, as did his companions, but something he did not understand surfaced in a question. 'How did you know we'd gone west an' was up this pass?'

Big Ben Albright smiled a little. 'Rangemen saw you. Once from a hell of a distance southward, and the last time, at the place where we got our last remounts, when they was up in the trees south of here. Those fellers had a pretty close look at the three of you.'

Jack ran a hand across his stubbly jaw and regarded the lawman. 'Why go to all this bother, Sheriff? We agreed to get out of the country.'

'You shot up some of Schultz's riders.'

Cal turned indignant. 'We didn't shoot up no one. We caught 'em, and one feller's horse fell with him and he got a busted leg. We *could* have shot 'em.'

Ben Albright regarded Cal Hunter for a moment, then turned as his possemen brought in three saddled, bridled horses, and the horses of their prisoners. He said nothing more until everyone was ready to swing up, then he pointed. 'You fellers ride ahead of us down out of here. If you think you can duck into the trees, go ahead and try it.'

As they headed back down toward open country Hugh looked to his left now and then as though the idea of making a break for it was in his mind, but by the time they reached open country he had not tried it, and after that it was too late.

The sun was on its way; visibility was about as it had been the previous late afternoon, but it was much colder. Neither of Albright's possemen said a word nor even seemed very interested in the prisoners. By the time the sun was up four additional horsemen appeared from southward. Albright halted, the newcomers regarded Hugh, Cal and Jack stonily, then one of them, a tall, thin man who

102

wore an ivory-handled sixgun, crossed both hands atop his horn and said, 'They can go on into Hammersville with you, Sheriff, if you need 'em.'

Ben Albright smiled. 'I'm obliged for the offer, Andy, but from here on I can herd 'em along . . . I appreciate you loanin' me two of your crew though.'

Thin, unsmiling Andy regarded the captives again, lifting his rein-hand as he did so. 'It's a long ride, Sheriff—plenty of places along the way,' then turned and led his riders back southward.

Cal waited until the rangemen were distant, then turned indignantly on Ben Albright. 'What's the damned fool think we are—highwaymen?'

Ben motioned with his gloved right hand. 'Ride on.' He had their weapons tied to his saddle. It gave him the appearance of being a one-man Mex army.

When the warmth came Ben allowed them to water their horses without dismounting, then kept them riding steadily throughout the entire day. They had a much more direct route to follow on the road than they had used on their way out of Brulé Valley, and Albright knew how to cover miles. They'd lope, then walk, then lope again. They rested in late afternoon when Albright was confident of reaching his destination before it got too dark, and while they were resting the animals and

103

Hugh asked Ben Albright why he was bringing them back, why he had gone to all that trouble, the big sheriff answered calmly.

'I told you. You can't just ride into this country, pick fights and act ornery, then just ride on again.'

Jack was rolling a smoke when he spoke. 'You knew Schultz would have his men out there when you turned us loose.'

Ben Albright shook his head. 'I figured he'd have someone waiting after sunrise. That's why I routed you out a couple of hours earlier.'

Jack lit up, gazing at the older man. 'Maybe. But seems to me if I knew someone for as long as you've known Mister Schultz, you'd figure him out. You'd know about how he'd do things.'

Albright did not argue. He did not have to. He was armed, they were not. As he pointed to the horses, meaning for them to get astride, he said, 'No. You boys can believe what you like, but I didn't think there'd be anyone out there so darned early.' Then, from the back of his horse, he also said, 'You're the ones that botched it, not me. Why did you stop at the Hatrack Hanson place? You said you'd leave the country straightaway. But you didn't, you wasted a lot of valuable time up there . . . And hell, you could have eluded Barton—instead you had to look for trouble with him. Boys, there's one kind of human beings I got no sympathy with—fools. Now string out there ahead of me and shut up. I missed two meals today and darned if I'm goin' to miss the third one.'

They could have argued, could have justified themselves through a longer discussion, but none of them wanted to do this, particularly when they saw the Hammersville rooftops up ahead. They were tired, and like Ben Albright, they had not eaten during this long, demoralising day. But as they came across the last couple of miles Jack twisted in the saddle to ask a question.

'What are we charged with, Sheriff? Scarin' a man's horse so that it fell with him?'

Ben Albright rode several yards before replying. He had been contemplating the Hammersville rooftops for a while now, and although he was unaccustomed to making such long and demanding pursuits, the aches, the hunger and the tiredness were mitigated by the success. There had been talk around the countryside the last couple of years about Ben Albright being a little old for his sheriffing job. He had just proved this was not true by making a record-breaking manhunt—successfully. Not only had he brought them back, he would appear in town doing it single-handedly. The talk would cease now.

Then he saw that the man who had spoken had given up expecting an answer, and gave him one nonetheless. 'I'll tell you what you're charged with, boys—*bank robbery*!'

All three men riding up ahead turned and stared. It was dusk now so Albright could see only their astonishment. Perhaps if there had been some daylight left he would also have seen their consternation.

Not another word was said until they were into town with lamp-light showing irregularly through the Hammersville area, and they swung off in the alley behind the liverybarn. Then Cal scowled at Ben Albright and said, 'Bank robbery! What in the hell are you talking about?'

The nightman took their animals, prudently kept silent as he stared at the unarmed, whisker-stubbled villainous-looking men Sheriff Albright used his sixgun to herd on up through and out front in the direction of the jailhouse. Later, after the horses had been cared for, the nightman hurried briskly up to the saloon to lay the groundwork for a legend. Everyone up there was impressed. In fact the nightman, who was not supposed to leave the liverybarn while he was on duty down there, got so many free drinks that by the time he started back to the barn he'd have had trouble finding his behind using both hands.

When Albright had his lamp lighted and went to the stove to stoke it up a little, Hugh and his partners exchanged a look. Then the lawman wordlessly had them empty their pockets into their hats, herded them down into the cell-room and locked them up. When they were safely under lock and bars he fished inside a coat pocket, brought forth three rumpled large squares of paper and read off the descriptions from each one of them. They were not accompanied by pictures, but the descriptions were good enough. He finished reading, shoved the dodgers back into a pocket, and said, 'Wolftown, Montana, is a hell of a distance. You'd have made it if you hadn't fooled away a lot of time after I let you out. Now—I'm glad you didn't make it. They got a three hundred dollar reward on each one of you.'

Cal protested. 'Wolftown, Montana? Where the hell is that? Those descriptions could cover every other rangerider you meet out in the roadway any damned day of the week, Sheriff.'

Albright gazed at Hugh Cole. 'Naw. Not as long as you fellers had this 'breed along. And what clinched it for me that you was fools was—not changing your names . . . I'll tell you what I think, because I've seen this time an' time again. Here's three rangeriders been workin' hard all their lives and gettin' nowhere. Frozen, baked, hurt, barely gettin' by for years—and they get enough and raid a bank—or a stagecoach, or sometimes a cowman's office at a ranch . . .' Albright stopped speaking, considered each of them in turn for a while, then curled his lip in pure contempt, said, 'Fools,' and stalked out of the cell-room on his way across the road before the caféman closed up for the night.

Behind him were three men whose despondency was not as great as their self-conscious chagrin. Everything Albright had said had been the truth. Jack rolled a smoke and perched upon the edge of his bunk. Cal paced, looking blackly into the settling gloom, and Hugh went over to lounge against the front wall of his cell. He was the first one to say something forthrightly which exacerbated the nerves of his partners.

'We *are* fools. There wasn't any reason for us to figure, because we didn't see anyone on our back-trail for a long while, that we'd be safe. Professional outlaws wouldn't have eaten breakfast nor looked at that lunger's thoroughbred horses. And they'd have explored the damned countryside too.'

Cal abruptly stopped pacing and went over to grip the bars. 'The saddlebags. Sure as hell he's goin' to open them and look in.'

Jack trickled smoke and considered the stone floor at his feet. 'I'll tell you what we did wrong,' he said musingly. 'We never should have got involved around here at all. Beginnin' with the poolhall, we never should have taken sides against *anyone*. We'd have made it but for that.'

Hugh turned and set his shoulders against the doorbars gazing at his partners. 'We can discuss this when we're old men sittin' in the

108

sun, somewhere. Right now, we got to figure what to do next.'

Cal's agitation made him irritable. It did not take very much to make Cal Hunter that way at his best, but now, with the prospect of never seeing his hoard of stolen greenbacks again he said, 'What we got to do next is chew our way through these bars. Or sprout wings and fly out of here when he fetches us back something to eat.' He snorted and glared through the bars at Hugh Cole. 'What we're goin' to do next, is set right here because we can't do nothin' else, and when a judge sets up court in Hammersville, we're goin' to get sent to prison . . . Hugh, you don't have to figure out what's goin' to happen next, it's already been figured out for us.'

It was so dark in the cell-room by the time Sheriff Albright got back with their pails of beans and coffee he had to light a lantern in the little dingy corridor before he could even see to shove the pails under their doors.

They were too disgruntled and demoralised to respond when he tried to strike up a conversation with them, turned their backs on him, and Ben shrugged, then departed for the night. By now, even *his* feet were aching.

CHAPTER ELEVEN

THE MONEY

It rarely mattered to rangemen what day of the week it was, unless they were employed by outfits which were within good riding-distance from a town. Then Saturday was important because Saturday night was their period for letting off steam; but for men like Hugh Cole, Jack Brunner and Cal Hunter, not only was it unimportant to them that their first day in the Hammersville jailhouse fell on a Sunday, it was equally unimportant to them that Sheriff Albright fed them early and did not appear in the cell-room again until high noon, and when he arrived that time he had another man with him.

They recognised the skinny individual despite his Church-going attire, and regarded him stonily; if they had not wasted time admiring his thoroughbred horses, they probably wouldn't be in jail now.

Ben Albright said, 'Half an hour,' to Leo Stanton, then left him standing in the dingy corridor gravely considering the prisoners. When the cell-room door closed behind the sheriff Stanton said, 'In my profession you learn to make judgments.' Then he said no more as the three men in their strap-steel cages continued to gaze at him in deep silence.

Stanton then said, 'My business is the law. I haven't worked at it since I left Chicago.'

Cal annoyedly said, 'I thought it was thoroughbred horses.'

Stanton's lean face showed a hint of a smile. 'That's my hobby. It's my second love. I've always loved horses—but to make a living something more is required. I'm a lawyer.'

The three fugitives studied Leo Stanton, and at least one of them began to feel a stirring of hope. Jack Brunner strolled to the front of his cell and held forth a hand. 'Give me your gun,' he said.

Stanton gave Jack look for look. 'I don't carry a pistol. I've rarely carried one. I wouldn't give it to you if I had one this morning. What possible good could you do for yourselves by shooting your way out of here?'

Cal, still using that annoyed tone, said, 'A lot of good for ourselves, mister—we could get out of this damned country.'

'You didn't manage that too successfully yesterday.'

'We didn't know Albright would be after us so hard.' Stanton considered Cal's unshaven, square-jawed face a moment, then spoke drily. 'You should have known it, if you're outlaws.'

Hugh spoke up. 'What brought you in here this morning?'

Stanton answered crisply. 'Church. My wife is a strong church-goer. Me? I came to execute a writ to have you released.'

Cal looked more sceptical than hopeful, but he too went to the front of his cell. 'All right, then go ahead and execute it, if that's what you call it.'

Stanton reached to an inside coat pocket and brought forth several folded papers. 'I have executed the writs. All I'm now required to do by law is serve them on the sheriff—and post bond for each one of you.' Stanton tapped the papers on his fingers. 'Do you each have fifty dollars?'

They did have. In fact they had that much left of their own, earned money. Jack nodded his head. 'Is that for you as our lawyer, or for the bail?'

'The bail. I won't charge you anything for my services. My reason for that, gents, is because neither you nor I like Walter Schultz.'

Hugh said, 'He'll burn you out, sure as hell. It's a wonder to me he hasn't done it already.'

'More likely,' grumbled Cal Hunter, 'he'll have you shot, *then* burned out.'

Leo Stanton's expression did not change. 'I don't think I'll serve these writs,' he said, looking thoughtful. 'The minute you walk out of here, he'll have some of his men hunt you down.'

'Up to now,' said Jack drily, 'when he's done that, it hasn't worked too well.'

Stanton stopped tapping the papers. 'From what I've heard, you fellers caught him

112

unprepared. Believe me—ask anyone around the countryside—no one ever catches Walter Schultz unprepared the next time.'

'We'll take our chances,' stated Cal. 'Just serve them damned papers, and we'll look after the other things.'

Stanton turned toward Hugh Cole. 'I suspected you weren't just itinerant rangemen when I first met you. Afterwards I was sure of it. Sheriff Albright showed me the wanted posters from up in Montana. It's one thing to buck Walter Schultz, and another thing to rob a bank. And it's not just that you'd forfeit your bail money by leaving the country, it is also that you'd put me in a very bad position.'

'You're already in one,' growled Cal. 'They shot your dog, didn't they? They want you off that land up in the hills they been usin' free, don't they?'

'I'm balancing on the raw edge now,' stated Leo Stanton. 'Having you escape from Brulé Valley because of something I did—serving these writs, for example—would put me over the edge. Not just with Sheriff Albright, but also with Mister Schultz and just about everyone else.'

Hugh had a small frown in place when he said, 'Just what in the hell did you come in here for; to show us how easy you could get us out of here—to tease us?'

The thin man considered an answer before offering it. 'I came in here because I know about that nine thousand dollars. I heard about it from Doctor Tillitson here in town when he rode out to the ranch yesterday to bring me some medicine for my consumption.'

Cal turned on the skinny man with a snarl. 'You don't get a red cent of that . . . That's why you come; to make us a trade—for our dollars you'll get us out of here. Mister, I'm beginnin' to have as much use for you as I have for that lousy lawman. I think he figured to get us killed by turning us out for Schultz's crew to run down. I think you'd take our money and arrange for us to get out—so's someone else could shoot us down.'

Hugh and Jack watched Leo Stanton's face, their expressions hinting that they might have found something in Cal's statement worth pondering. Then the skinny, solemn man made a statement that obliterated all their other thoughts.

He said, 'I don't want any part of that stolen money. If I had wanted it, I'd have gotten it without you three knowing anything about it. *Doctor Tillitson has your nine thousand dollars.*'

For five seconds there was not a sound inside the jailhouse. Finally, Hugh said, 'How did he get it?'

'He was in the saloon last night when the hostler from the liverybarn came busting in to say he'd just cared for your three horses, and that Sheriff Albright had just taken you up to the jailhouse . . . Doc knew who you were,

114

Sheriff Albright had told him yesterday morning when he was saddling up to go after you. It's doubtful that the sheriff had the time to tell anyone else. So—last night as soon as the hostler talked his head off up at the saloon, Doc ran down to the liverybarn and searched your saddlebags. What fascinates me is why Ben Albright had not already done that.'

Neither Jack, Hugh nor Cal were fascinated by the lawman's oversight, or whatever it was, they were staring through the bars at Leo Stanton, gradually turning furious at what the medical practitioner had done.

Cal's anger burst loose. 'When I get out of here I'm goin' to hunt down that old bastard and break both his arms so's that old devil won't be able to rob nobody else's saddlebags for a long time.'

Stanton resumed tapping the papers against his hand. 'Just be quiet and listen to me,' he said, then waited to see if he would be obeyed. He was; even agitated Cal Hunter had nothing to say. 'You won't get that money back, resign yourselves to that.' Stanton paused, then said, 'I talked to Doctor Tillitson just before church. I told him I was going to represent you against Walter Schultz. He leaned over and whispered in my ear what he knew and what he had done—got your stolen money . . . After church we sat in the shade and conferred.'

Jack was impatient. 'What the hell are you leadin' up to?'

115

Stanton stopped tapping the papers. 'This; Sheriff Albright sent a letter by stagecoach up to Foleyton where the nearest telegraph is—at the railroad stop. The message is to be telegraphed to Montana. By now it's already up there. They will send a lawman down to take you three into custody, extradite you to Montana and you'll be tried up there—if you don't get lynched first.'

'That'll take a month,' growled Cal, and Leo Stanton contradicted him. 'It won't take more than three or four days. Albright told them to send a lawman by train down to Foleyton and he'd have a stage pick him up there and fetch him down to Hammersville. He could be here in three days, four days at the most.'

In a subsiding voice Cal said, 'It took us a danged month.'

Stanton ignored that to gaze steadily at Jack when he spoke again. 'Doc and I will offer the Montana lawman a trade—they are to drop charges in exchange for getting their money back—and *then* I'll serve the writ, you will be free men—and targets for Walter Schultz.' Into the long silence which followed the unfolding of this plan, Leo Stanton heard someone enter the office from the roadway, and, assuming it was the sheriff, he lowered his voice and spoke again, rapidly. 'Not a word of this to anyone. Anyone at all! Think it over. I'll be back in an hour.'

Hugh stepped up against the bars. 'Why?'

116

he demanded curtly.

Stanton was turning away when he spat an answer. 'I already told you. Anyone who is an enemy of Walter Schultz is a friend of mine—and also of Doctor Tillitson.'

Ben Albright came part-way down the corridor. 'I thought I told you a half hour,' he snarled, and Stanton walked up past Albright into the office.

Fifteen minutes elapsed before the sheriff returned to his cell-room. It did not require that much time for Jack and Hugh to get Cal Hunter down from his pacing rage. But it nearly took that much time because, although Cal could certainly realise there was no alternative available to them but to agree with the Tillitson-Stanton scheme unless they chose to go to prison, Cal had developed a very personal and vested interest in the money he had suffered considerably for, and lay awake at night dreaming of spending.

By the time Ben Albright came back, Cal was stretched full length upon his wall-bunk and neither looked around nor opened his mouth as the lawman said, 'There's a deputy coming for you three from Montana. He's goin' to get extradition papers . . . Where did you cache the nine thousand dollars?'

Hugh was easing down upon the edge of his bunk when he answered. 'We spent it in wild livin' on our way south.'

'No, you didn't,' exclaimed Albright. 'The

117

route you boys used to get down here don't have any towns along it where a man could do any wild living. Where is it? Listen to me—once that feller from Montana gets here, you're finished, all three of you. Maybe, if I handed him back that money, he'd put in a good word for you back in Montana when they put you on trial.'

'Yeah,' muttered Cal still without moving or looking around. 'He'd put in such a good word they wouldn't lynch us, they'd just sentence us to life in prison.'

'Well, what the hell do you expect?' demanded Ben Albright. 'You robbed that blasted bank, didn't you? Now make it easier for me as well as for yourselves—where did you cache the money?'

Jack leaned with his shoulders against the steel bars at his back and eyed Ben Albright. 'We'll need somethin' to get started with when we get out of prison,' he said, and began to scratch. 'Sheriff, no one's goin' to do us any favours, including you.'

Albright thought a moment before speaking again. 'I can do *someone* a favour, cowboy, I can turn you out of here and let Walt Schultz have you.'

'We can't post bail,' stated Jack.

'Yes you can. You've each got a little more'n fifty dollars in your hats up in my office. I'll designate it bail money.'

Hugh had been regarding the lawman

118

throughout all this, and now said, 'Why don't you make up your mind whose side of the fence you're on? Couple days back you tried to help us escape old Schultz. Today you're talkin' about lettin' him have a few shots at us.'

Albright said, 'The money. Just tell me where you cached the damned bank money.'

Cal growled again from the prone position he had assumed on his bunk. 'Go to hell,' he muttered, and heaved up onto his side as though he intended to sleep.

Ben Albright looked from one of them to the other, then turned away as he spoke. 'All right. It's up to you. If they lynch you just remember that if you'd cooperated with me, it wouldn't have happened.'

No one spoke until the cell-room door closed behind Albright, then Hugh offered an opinion. 'I like Stanton's idea best. Albright's way we'd still go back to Montana.'

For a long time neither of Hugh's partners had anything to say. In fact until shortly before Albright appeared, looking grim and hostile, to bring their evening meal, there was no further discussion. Then Jack sat up looking to his right and left into the adjoining cells.

'By now sure as hell old Schultz knows we're in here an' that we robbed a bank. I wouldn't bet a plugged penny that even when that Montanan shows up for us, and gets us out of here, Schultz won't know about it and be out there waiting.'

It was an unpleasant thing to contemplate. Neither Hugh nor Cal had anything to say until Ben had brought their meal, had glared in at them, then had stamped his way back up to light his office lamp in dogged silence.

They had finished supper and were sitting disconsolately in their cells when the sheriff returned, big-booted feet making a hard, solid sound as he advanced down to the front of their cells. He had someone with him, and this man did not make that much noise when he moved, because he was careful when he walked.

It was beefy, cold-eyed Walter Schultz, his round, thick-featured face made to look even more coarse and brutal in the bad lamplight.

The sheriff stood back, watching, as Schultz peered into each cell, then hitched over to lean upon the bars of Hugh Cole's cell. He had good reason to single Hugh out. He said, 'So you're a damned rotten bank robber, are you? I figured you fellers were some kind of renegade the first time I put eyes on you.'

Hugh's black gaze was like obsidian as he stared back. 'You never figured anything, you old goat,' he said, and when Schultz raised one powerful hand to grip the bars as though he would uproot them, Hugh continued to stare out into the corridor. 'What did you bring him in here for, Sheriff?'

Ben Albright's eyes glinted like wet steel beneath the smoking old corridor-lantern. He did not answer.

Schultz said, 'You want to get out of Hammersville alive? Tell Ben where you hid that bank money.'

Hugh curled his lip, not at Walt Schultz but at the equally big and beefy man behind him. 'You're wasting your time, Sheriff. Get this old lump of carrion out of here so's we can go to sleep.'

Hugh turned his face to the wall and left both Schultz and Albright to stand there looking at him. Schultz hitched around. Jack and Cal were silently staring out into the corridor. Cal snarled at Schultz. 'You remind me of a teller named Babcock I knew once. You're nothin' but a tinhorn, know-nothing, would-be know-it-all, phony son of a bitch.'

Walter Schultz's beefy large hand, curled around his cane-handle, whitened. 'That,' he told Cal Hunter, 'just bought you a gravestone.' He glared, then hitched around to stamp angrily back up to the office. Up there, as Ben Albright was closing the door to bar it, Schultz turned on him viciously.

'You damned fool, Ben. They don't scare. I *told* you that at the saloon. You used me, Ben. And by gawd you tried to let those men slip past me the morning you turned 'em out. I want to tell you something—you've taken the wrong side this time. You won't be the first lawman I've busted out of here. I'm going to bury those three bastards and so help me you'd

121

better not get in the way!'

Schultz stamped out and left the door open behind himself. As Ben went over to close it, he decided that what Schultz had said about his bank-robber not scaring worth a damn, was correct. He also told himself, on his way over to the desk to sit down, that he had made a blunder in taking Walt Schultz down there to confront those prisoners.

But he wanted to find that bank money. It suddenly struck him to rush down to the liverybarn and go through their saddlebags. He sprang up with more haste than he'd used in arising from a chair in years.

The nightman shook his head when Ben shouldered him aside and pushed into the harness room. The moment he began fumbling with a saddlebag the nightman said, 'You're too late, Mister Albright. Someone else has already gone through them bags.'

Ben turned. 'Who?'

'I got no idea, Mister Albright. All I know is that last night I went up to the saloon for a few minutes, and them flaps was buckled down, and when I got back to make me some black coffee, I noticed them flaps was unbuckled and some of the stuff that'd been in them three sets of bags was on the floor . . . Care for a cup of coffee?'

'No! Who was in here, damn it all?'

The nightman recoiled a little. It was a small, cluttered room and Ben Albright was a large man even when anger did not make him seem larger. 'I honest to gawd don't have no idea, Sheriff. I wasn't gone awful long, but when I come back . . . I honest to gawd got no idea who it was.'

CHAPTER TWELVE

BEN ALBRIGHT'S PROBLEMS

Ben Albright lost five pounds between Sunday and Wednesday. That was a signal that he was worried and anxious; but actually a man as large and heavy as Ben was, could lose five pounds almost any four days he chose to do so without worrying. But Ben *was* worried. He had pleaded, tried cold logic, and had even hinted at a compromise if the prisoners would tell him where the bank loot was hidden. He finally told them he would not bring any more food to the jailhouse until they told him what he wanted to know, but when the café man noticed that the sheriff was not ordering food for his prisoners, and mentioned it to Frank Tillitson, the medical practitioner came stamping into the jailhouse office red-eyed and bushy-tailed.

Ben weathered the verbal lashing from behind his desk. When Doc was through he said, 'Frank, I brought those men in without help, and set some kind of record in ridin' from here out to Overland Pass to catch them by surprise in their bedrolls at night.'

The wispy, wiry older man made a slight sniffing sound. 'Wonderful. And you want a medal for that.'

'No, damn it; I just want that nine thousand dollars they robbed that Montana bank of, to complete the manhunt. Without it I'm goin' to look like I only half did my job.'

Frank Tillitson jerked a chair around, straddled it and stared at Ben Albright. 'Ben, you get paid to run down outlaws. That's your job. What you did by making that long ride and bringin' them back was make yourself look like what the Town Council and everyone else pays you to do. Who said you got to find hidden money too? That's up to the Montana authorities. You did your job, and I guess you did it right well. That's all anyone expects you to do.'

Albright relaxed a little, beginning to feel somewhat mollified. 'All the same . . .'

'How much bounty money is on those men, Ben?'

'Three hundred dollars each.'

'That'll be yours, won't it?'

'Yes, but . . .'

'But my butt! You did your job. Leave it to the Montanans to find that damned money—if it's around.' Frank Tillitson put his head slightly to one side, which made him resemble a small, wiry bird more than ever. 'I saw you bring Walt Schultz in here last Sunday.'

Ben began to redden. 'What of it? What I got to do in the performance of my job as lawman is my business. Frank, what have you been doing lately, keeping tabs on me?'

Doctor Tillitson reared back as though to arise from his chair. Instead of replying to the lawman's question he said, 'I want to see the hand of that feller who busted Carl's face an' cracked his ribs.' Then Doctor Tillitson stood up facing Albright as though challenging him.

The sheriff did not move for a few moments, then he leaned, picked up his key-ring and stood up. 'There's nothing wrong with his hand. It's a little puffy and blue is all. It's not even very swollen.'

Tillitson cocked his head again. 'A little puffy and blue? Those are signs of blood poisoning. Are you going to let me see that man or not?'

Albright's colour deepened. He considered the smaller man with an expression of strong distaste showing on his face. Then he growled. 'Come along.' At the cell-room door he frowned. 'How are you goin' to make a bandage, you don't have your little satchel?'

'I'll make an examination first,' retorted the doctor, 'then, if it's necessary I'll come back with my satchel.'

The prisoners had shaved the day before, but otherwise they did not look very presentable. Those new clothes they had bought some time back in Hammersville, looked even worse than their old flea-infested attire had looked.

Ben Albright leaned down to unlock Jack Brunner's cell and hold the door as Frank

126

Tillitson entered, then, still wearing that expression of distaste, the lawman returned to his office. He did not intend to stand out there waiting for the doctor to complete his examination and be glared at by the three prisoners.

Frank Tillitson stepped to the front bars, looked up where Ben had gone, then, satisfied, he turned and said, 'Leo Stanton couldn't return. It's a hell of a buggy-drive back to their place in the foothills and his wife—'

Cal was on his feet gripping the bars and glaring through them. 'You old bastard, where is our money?'

Frank Tillitson turned, regarded Cal's expression for a moment, then said, 'It's safe. I hid it. Mister, you'll never see your share of it, so you better get accustomed to that.' He paused to range a look at Hugh and Jack, then he spoke again in a less brusque manner. 'It's up to you boys; do you want Leo and me to bargain with the feller they send down here to take you back, or do you want to keep the money and spend the rest of your lives, or a darned good part of them, in prison?'

Doc knew the answer he would receive before he asked the question, and Hugh Cole affirmed it for him. 'Bargain. Give him back the nine thousand dollars—providin' he leaves us here and goes back to Montana.'

Tillitson shook his head. 'That's not good enough. You've got to have a complete pardon. They've got to agree to that, and send it down here in writing.'

Cal growled. 'That'll take months.'

Tillitson had one of his pithy answers for that. 'You can spend months here in the Hammersville jailhouse, or you can spend years in the Montana Territorial Prison.'

Jack looked over at Cal, and scowled. Cal subsided, but his look of outrage did not diminish very much as Jack said, 'They can have their money back in exchange for pardoning us. All right, Doctor. Anything else?'

Tillitson advanced upon Jack. 'Sit on that bunk and hold out your sore hand. That's why I said I had to see you. Sit down.'

Jack sat, Doctor Tillitson examined the hand carefully, told Jack to make a fist, then examined some more, and finally shrugged as he turned back toward the cell door. 'It's all right. But anyone ought to know better than to hit someone that hard. You could have put Carl to sleep with half that much force.' At the doorway he twisted until his eyes fell upon Cal. 'You, mister, better learn to keep your mouth shut at least half the time. A temper right now is likely to get you in trouble for the next twenty years.'

Cal stiffened, but before he could speak Hugh had a question for Tillitson. 'You are a friend of the sheriff's and you got to live with Walter Schultz. What happens when they both find out what you and Stanton have been up to—especially about you takin' that money and hiding it?'

The wiry, leathery-faced older man grinned. 'Why, I suppose Walter will want to shoot me and Ben will want to stamp me into the dirt.' He continued to grin as he marched out of Jack's cell, locked it after himself, removed the big brass key and went hiking with a springy step up to the sheriff's office. As he tossed the key atop Ben's desk he smiled at the large man. 'His hand's not too bad. There might be a little infection, the hand felt a little warm to me, Ben. I'll look in on him tomorrow—and Ben—if you don't feed them I'm going to demand a meeting of the Town Council.'

Albright was leaning over the desk like a bear. He regarded Tillitson from hostile eyes. 'Someday, Frank, you're going to go too far.'

The doctor kept smiling all the way to the door. Over there, he turned, still smiling, to make an offer. 'I'll stand you to a nightcap over at the saloon after supper . . . By the way, Ben, a Montana lawman came into town on the afternoon stage. He's up at the rooming-house getting the dust sluiced off . . . See you at the saloon tonight.'

Albright continued to lean there until the door closed and for a moment or two afterwards, then he grabbed his hat, put it on and stood up staring at the cell-room door trying to decide whether or not to go back down there and try one more time to get his prisoners to tell him where their cache was. In the end he gave up the idea; they would be no more cooperative now than they had been until now—and until today they had at least had food in their bellies.

He went over to the café, growled for the pails of prisoner grub, took them back with him to the cell-room, and as he was shoving the little pails beneath the doors he decided to be a reasonable man. As he stood up he said, 'Listen, fellers—time's run out. The lawman from Montana is here in town. Make him a decent offer. Do it for your own sakes. It don't matter to me anymore. I caught you, that's all I was supposed to do.'

Hugh sauntered over to pick up his pair of pails. 'When'll he come down here?' he asked, reaching for the pails then straightening up.

'In the morning,' Albright replied, and thought he knew what Hugh had in mind, so he also said, 'You got that much time left. Give me a decision in the morning, and if it's the right one, I'll do what I can to help you.'

Not another word was said. Ben went back up to his office, let go a big, rattling sigh, and left the jailhouse on his way in the direction of the roominghouse.

Frank Tillitson had been right, Ben had not been required to accomplish any more than he had done; he had made a spectacular capture. Already, people nodded to him and waved and smiled, and acted more respectful than they had been acting toward him the last year or two.

But it would certainly look much better if he could throw down that Montana bank loot with a flourish when the Montana lawman came to the jailhouse in the morning. That would be the icing on the cake.

The iron-eyed, large, greying woman who owned and operated the roominghouse stood squarely in her front doorway the way she always did, and did not smile when Ben asked about a Montana lawman. She jerked a thumb and said, 'He didn't say he was a lawman, Sheriff. He just said he wanted a clean room, a towel, a chunk of soap, and the use of the bath-house out back.'

'Is he still out there?'

'No. He's in his room.' The woman stepped aside and pointed with the same thumb. 'Number seven.'

'What's his name?'

The woman let her hand fall. 'Kenniston. I'd say that it was probably his real name too. No one would try to spell a name like that unless it really belonged to him . . . Number seven.'

Ben followed the large woman down her threadbare hall runner. She continued on down the hall and Ben turned to roll a big set of knuckles over the closed door of room number seven.

The man who opened the door was medium-sized and getting a little thin on top. He was dressed more like a townsman than a rangeman and as Albright introduced himself and made his swift, initial assessment, he could find no sign of a shellbelt nor gun beneath Kenniston's coat.

The Montanan waved Albright into the room. There, lying on the bed, was a pearl-handled sixgun, so black it looked new. But the carved holster and shellbelt did not look new. They looked expensive and more ornate than Ben had seen in a long time, but they were not new.

The Montanan said, 'Have a seat, Sheriff. My first name is John.' Kenniston picked up the belt, used a professional flourish to whirl it around under his coat, and as he buckled it he kept looking at Sheriff Albright. 'I was goin' to have supper then come over to the jailhouse. How are the prisoners?'

'Ornery,' stated the sheriff, admiring the Prince Albert coat and handsome black boots of John Kenniston. They either preferred their lawmen to look elegant up in Montana, or this one was in a class by himself. He still did not look like a lawman to Ben Albright. At least not like the usual cow-township lawman. But as he moved and the ivory-stocked Colt moved gracefully, as though it were a part of him, Ben began to think that John Kenniston looked the part of a very good gunfighter. Ben said, 'You

132

can have 'em in the morning. You can send back my cuffs and leg-irons when you get up there with them.'

Kenniston turned, still looking very affable. 'You have the money?'

Ben shifted position a little. 'No. Not yet, but I've been sweatin' them to find out where they cached it.' He raised his eyes and saw the affability in John Kenniston's face beginning to fade a little. Without much confidence in the words, Ben also said, 'In the morning they'll most likely tell me where it is.'

Kenniston nodded his head in a gentle manner. 'I reckon they'll tell you, Sheriff. If not, and you'd care to go over to the poolhall for a half-hour, they'll tell me.'

Ben began to get an odd feeling about this handsome, friendly man with the pearl-handled sixgun. He muttered, 'We'll see. We'll see in the morning . . . Anything I can do for you while you're in Hammersville?'

'No thanks, Sheriff. I'll have some supper and maybe a drink or two, then turn in . . . I'll see you in the morning over at your jailhouse.'

Ben closed the door after himself and walked slowly back out to the front porch. He had not really cottoned very much to Kenniston even before the man had made that remark about getting information from prisoners when there was no other lawman around.

It was common practice, Ben had known

133

that for years, but he had never indulged in it.

It was one thing to whang the whey out of someone in a fair fight, and it was something altogether different to beat hell out of someone who was unarmed in a jail cell, to get information from them.

He turned back toward the main centre of town, and nearly collided with Red Barton and one of the other riders who worked for Walter Schultz in the shadows out front of the saddle and harness works. He glared at them. A lot of small things were beginning to bother Ben. 'You're a long ride from home for so late in the day,' he said, without making it sound like much of a greeting.

Barton was caught unprepared by the hint of hostility, but recovered swiftly. 'We came in with the feller who had his leg busted by those outlaws you got in the cells. Anything wrong with that, Ben?'

'Yeah. They didn't bust that man's leg, his horse busted it. How long you goin' to be in town?'

Barton began to frown in bewilderment. 'Not long. Just until Doc looks over the splints, and then we got to take back some more of Walt's heart medicine . . . Something bothering you?'

Albright thought about his answer before offering it. 'Yeah. A half-dozen damned things,' he said, and stalked on past in the direction of the saloon. After he had passed

134

along, the cowboy with Schultz's rangeboss rubbed the point of his jaw as he watched Sheriff Albright's bear-sized body moving away. 'What you reckon it is, Red?'

Barton had no idea, but he did not like it, so he said, 'Let's go get that damned medicine, get astride and head for home.'

'Without a stop at the waterin' hole first?'

Barton considered that answer more carefully, then reluctantly said, 'The hell with it. Albright went in down there. We got some whiskey in the bunkhouse. Let's go.'

CHAPTER THIRTEEN

MATTERS OF JUDGEMENT

Frank Tillitson was at a little table near the stove when Sheriff Albright entered the saloon. Frank already had a bottle so all Ben took with him to the table was a shot glass, and as he eased down under the examining eyes of the medical doctor and reached for the bottle, Frank said, 'You talked to the Montanan?'

Ben downed his jolt before answering. 'Yeah. Did you get a good look at him, Frank?'

'No. I never saw the man at all. One of the stage company hostlers told me he'd arrived lookin' for the roominghouse. Why?'

Ben slumped down in the chair to get comfortable. 'Pearl handles on his Colt, and one of those black, long coats like undertakers wear, and shiny boots.' Ben shot Tillitson a sidelong glance. 'Not that there's anything wrong with dressin' like that, but it's been a while since I've seen a fancy-Dan lawman.'

Frank reached for the bottle. He'd already had a shot before the sheriff had arrived. In fact, Frank had not been sure Albright would take him up on his offer over at the jailhouse because they had not parted smiling. He poured, then sat there looking at the little shot glass. 'Maybe he's one of those gunfightin' lawmen, Ben. Is he a disagreeable feller?'

'No. Fact is he's downright polite and smilin' and pleasant. But he's got a cold set of eyes on him . . . Oh well; he can have his prisoners in the morning, and get 'em out of here on the early stage. Be done with it. Have it over with.'

'What about the money?'

Big Ben Albright looked across the table. 'I don't have it. I'll make one more effort in the morning to get them to tell me where it's hidden, then to hell with it. I'm sick of this whole damned mess.'

Tillitson finally reached for the full jolt-glass. Ten minutes later he left Sheriff Albright sitting in the pleasant, warm and relaxing atmosphere of the saloon, which, on a Wednesday night, did very little business, and for that reason the place was quiet.

Frank Tillitson went up to his residence, which also served as his office and clinic, and was making a pot of coffee when a horseman arrived out in the alley, tied his horse to the fence back there and walked up to knock with a gloved fist on Frank's kitchen door.

It was Leo Stanton bundled into a sheepskin coat and wearing a hat and muffler as though it were bitterly cold out, but actually it was not as cold as it usually was.

Tillitson pointed to a kitchen chair at his table and said, 'Coffee'll be ready directly,' then told Stanton what Ben had said about the Montana lawman. Leo listened, loosened his

137

heavy coat because it was warm with the kitchen stove fired up, and removed his hat. But he did not remove his gloves and when the coffee cup was placed in front of him he still did not remove them.

They sat quietly for a while, sipping coffee, before Stanton said, 'You got the money, Doctor?'

Frank nodded and patted the front of his rumpled old coat. 'Yes. Drink it down and we'll go hunt up the Montanan. I forgot to ask Ben what his name is.' Frank pushed an empty cup away and smiled thinly. 'But that won't matter a lot, will it?'

They paused out front and Stanton re-buttoned his sheep-pelt coat. Frank watched Leo do this and asked a professional question. 'You been coughin' much lately?'

Stanton finished gazing up and down the roadway before replying. 'Almost none at all. That's a good sign, isn't it?'

Frank struck out across the road toward the side-street where the roominghouse stood. 'The best sign of all, next to gainin' weight . . . You'll make it, Leo. Just don't catch a cold. Get a lot of sleep and eat hot food and plenty of greens. I've told you all that before.'

They turned in past the sagging roominghouse gate and this time when someone knocked on her door the large, square-jawed woman who owned the structure opened the door with less of a challenging

138

attitude. She closed the door after them and answered Doctor Tillitson's question with a jerk of her thumb. 'Room number seven. He's in there. He came back from supper about ten, fifteen minutes ago . . . Doctor, you know that pain in my back? It's startin' up again. I been trying to get a little time so's I could come over and see you but runnin' this place is like tryin' to herd wild mules.'

Frank patted the big woman's arm as he began edging along the corridor. 'Make the time, Helen. Let some of the work go, and make the time. You only get one back and if you don't favour it you'll have to let all the work go eventually.' He led Leo Stanton to the door of John Kenniston's room, and knocked.

The Montanan was without his Prince Albert coat when he opened the door, but the handsome blued gun with the pearl handles was in its place around his middle. He smiled, eyebrows lifting in enquiry. Frank introduced Leo Stanton, then mentioned his own name. He did not state Stanton's occupation until after they were in the room with the door closed and Kenniston was pointing toward places for them to sit down.

Then Kenniston's gaze at the consumptive lawyer brightened with renewed curiosity. 'A lawyer?' he said. 'I didn't have any idea they'd have one in a place like Hammersville. Cow-towns usually have a marshal or sheriff and that's about it . . . Well, gents, what can I

139

do for you?'

Leo Stanton spoke first. 'To begin with, Mister Kenniston, I'd like to know whether you're a marshal, a sheriff, or what?'

The affable Montanan smiled a little and dug in a pocket of his frock coat where it was hanging from a wooden peg on the wall, came back with a little gold badge on his palm and said, 'I'm a special policeman for the banking protective association of Montana. I'm authorised to operate in any township in Montana Territory, and to represent the legal authorities when they authorise it.' He went to the room's single bed and sat upon the edge of it, no longer smiling but looking affable. When Frank and Leo Stanton exchanged a look, Kenniston's smile returned. 'Would you like to see my legal authorisation to represent Montana law?' Without awaiting a reply he returned to the frock coat and pulled out several documents from an inside pocket. He handed one to Leo Stanton. 'Signed by the governor,' he said, and when Leo had finished reading, Kenniston handed him three more papers. 'Orders of extradition for Cole, Hunter and Brunner.' Then the Montanan returned to the edge of the bed and waited. Stanton handed the documents to Frank, and while Tillitson was reading them, Leo said, 'Mister Kenniston, I represent Brunner, Hunter and Cole.' Then he paused while the Montanan inclined his head. Kenniston said, 'You want to

140

block extradition and have them brought to trial down here.'

Stanton shook his head. 'No. What I want to do is make you an offer.'

Kenniston's pale eyes drew out into a narrowed look of shrewdness. 'Go ahead, Mister Stanton.'

'The nine thousand dollars returned to you in exchange for a written pardon for my clients.'

Clearly, John Kenniston had encountered this situation before. 'So they can rob another bank,' he said, without sounding disagreeable.

'They never robbed a bank before, Mister Kenniston. They're rangemen. They won't rob another bank.'

'You can guarantee that, Mister Stanton?'

Frank Tillitson answered. 'I can guarantee it.'

Kenniston's eyes shifted. 'How, Doctor? An outlaw's word isn't worth the breath they use to utter it.'

'You're talking about outlaws, Mister Kenniston. I'm talkin' about three damned fools who have had their lesson.'

Kenniston looked from one of his visitors to the other, then said, 'Where is the nine thousand dollars?'

Doctor Tillitson said, 'Where is the pardon?'

Kenniston laughed. 'In the pocket of my coat over yonder.'

Frank and Leo Stanton stared at the

amiable man with the elegant sidearm.

'You—came down here prepared to trade?' asked Leo Stanton, and the business-like Montanan shrugged powerful shoulders. 'I represent banking interests, first of all. Secondly, I represent Montana law. I didn't think you'd have a telegraph office down here. Darned few cow-towns do have them, and I don't like waiting a couple of weeks for letters to pass back and forth . . . Gents, I've been through this ten dozen times in my career. I don't arrive in a place like Hammersville without being prepared for anything—and that includes pardoning or gunfighting . . . The pardons have been signed by the Governor. There is one stipulation: If any of those men, Hunter, Cole or Brunner, ever return to Montana, they will go to prison.'

The medical practitioner and the lawyer sat in silence until John Kenniston asked about the money again, then Frank said, 'Show me the pardons.'

Kenniston went to his coat and this time when he returned he had three crisp folded papers in his right hand. He held them out as he spoke. 'Does Sheriff Albright know what you are doing?'

Frank took the papers, handed them to Stanton, looked up and shook his head. 'No. And he'll be fit to be tied when he finds out.'

Kenniston stood looking steadily down at Frank Tillitson. 'Where is the money?'

142

Frank unbuttoned his shirt, felt inside for the string-tied packet of brown paper, drew it forth and handed it to Kenniston. Without a word the Montanan returned to the bed, broke the string, rifled through the greenbacks, then began systematically to count them.

Leo finished reading about the time the Montanan finished counting. Stanton let go a big sigh of relief and faced his companion. 'I wasn't prepared for this, Doctor.'

Kenniston was re-wrapping the nine thousand dollars and did not look up when he said, 'Most people aren't, but in my trade, gents, we do it regularly.' He went over and stowed the packet into an inside coat pocket, then turned and unsmilingly eyed his visitors. 'Maybe you've figured this out and maybe you haven't, but, gents, Cole, Brunner and Hunter are in the clear now—and you two are in trouble. You were withholding stolen money from the authorities—in this case, Sheriff Albright. He can charge you with complicity, jug you, and bring you to trial—and Montana won't be interested.'

Kenniston returned to the edge of the bed and sat down again. 'I'll take the morning stage north. You boys had better be very good friends of Sheriff Albright.' Kenniston smiled again, eyeing his visitors. 'Lawyer, you had to know about complicity.'

Leo Stanton had indeed known about being accessories. He had also known—or had *thought* he knew—that Ben Albright was neither a vindictive nor vengeful man. 'It's not Albright who worries me,' he told the Montanan, 'it's a bullying old cowman named Walter Schultz. He wanted Cole, Brunner and Hunter either shot, lynched or sent to prison . . . And he wants me off my land because he's been using it for his cattle.'

John Kenniston listened, smiled, then arose and paced to the door. 'I wish you luck,' he said, and held the door open. He was finished in Hammersville. He did not like cow-towns; he did not particularly like cowmen either, although he had started out in life as a rangeman. As Frank and Leo arose to depart, Kenniston offered a parting scrap of advice. 'Make a trade, gents. You won't tell how you hoodwinked him to get the money, if he'll just turn your friends loose and see that they leave Brulé Valley. He's a lawman. They got reputations to protect.'

Out in front of the roominghouse again, Leo Stanton paused to look back, then to shake his head. 'Kenniston is a professional, for a fact. I had no idea they were that progressive up in Montana.'

Frank shoved both hands into trouser-pockets and started walking in the direction of the main section of town. 'The hell with Montana and Mister Kenniston,' he said. 'We're not up there, we're down here, and we got Ben Albright to deal with, not John

144

Kenniston . . . How good a case can Ben make of us being accessories?'

'He can do it, Doctor. But he'll have to subpoena Kenniston to come back down here and testify that we had that money in our possession, and that we gave it to him, knowing it was stolen, and also knowing that it was withholding evidence to have it in our possession without letting Albright know we had it.'

Frank stopped where the side-street and Hammersville's main roadway converged. There were lights at the saloon, the liverybarn and the jailhouse. He stood gazing longest at the lights in the jailhouse. 'Kenniston wouldn't return to testify,' he said, and squared up his thin shoulders. 'Ben's down there in his office.'

They stood a long while gazing at the lighted, barred, front-wall window of the jailhouse. Eventually Frank said, 'Well, hell; we can do it now, or we can wait until Kenniston is gone, then do it. I'd suggest we give Kenniston a hell of a big head-start.'

Stanton agreed. They struck out for Doctor Tillitson's residence.

The night was still warm. So warm in fact that, as they walked along, Tillitson twice paused to glance upwards. But the sky was clear, every star was glowing, there were no clouds as far as he could see, and he stopped wondering whether it would rain or not as they pushed through his little front gate bound for

145

the kitchen where that coffee was waiting.

Inside, as he hung his hat and ran crooked fingers through his greying mane, Frank said, 'You better lie over. I got plenty of blankets and extra rooms. We can watch the morning stage pull out, then have breakfast to be fortified, and walk down to the jailhouse.'

Leo Stanton loosened his coat, stuffed his muffler and gloves into a pocket and followed Doctor Tillitson out to the kitchen where Frank turned up the table-lamp then went to test the coffeepot. From over there with his back to Leo he said, 'I went into this like a damned fool. A man should never decide to do something out of emotion . . . I dislike Walter Schultz very much. Those three cowboys bucked him, beat him, and humiliated him.' Frank took two full coffee cups to the table where Stanton was sitting. 'I approved of how they beat Walt. When they were brought back to town, I knew damned well Walt would be waiting—and he'll still be waiting. He's got to break them or be the laughing-stock of Brulé Valley . . . Be careful, that damned coffee is hot . . . I went all through this mess simply on emotion . . . I'm sixty-eight years old. You'd sure think I'd have better sense than to act like that, wouldn't you?'

Leo Stanton regarded the steaming coffee in front of him without commenting for a long while. But eventually he responded. 'I was a dying man when I came out here, Doctor, and

146

I'll still probably never fully recover from tuberculosis. When a man awakens each morning and retires each night with death beside him, he doesn't think the same way he thought when he was healthy and with no ideas about death at all . . .' Stanton's eyes came up slowly to fix themselves upon his host across the kitchen table. 'I hadn't thought about this before, but I've thought about it quite a bit recently. An inflexible law is responsible for an inflexible society. Life is not very long at its best. And I'll agree with you, emotional involvement in anything is likely to produce bad judgments. But *I* got a second chance, didn't I? Cole, Hunter and Brunner have the same right, haven't they? Life is too short to force people, who make one mistake, to use up a big part of it as punishment . . . I thought about this before I agreed to work with you on this. Maybe we were both too emotionally involved, but I'll tell you something, Frank— I'd do it again tomorrow, if I had to.'

Leo Stanton hoisted the cup, sipped black coffee, then shoved up to his feet. 'Where do I bed down?' He waited until his host had finished his coffee and was ready to lead the way, then Stanton also said, 'And it's not going to be just Sheriff Albright.'

He did not elaborate. He did not have to, Frank Tillitson was nodding his head in understanding as he led the way, lamp in hand.

CHAPTER FOURTEEN

A DEAD MAN!

They were waiting up the road when the north-bound stage pulled out of Hammersville. The sun was barely showing, there were cold shadows, Stanton was bundled inside his sheep-hide coat and was wearing both his muffler and gloves. Doc Tillitson—who'd had the good sense to fortify himself against the chill with Irish coffee before leaving his residence—had both hands in his trouser pockets, his hat dumped upon the back of his head, and was wearing his baggy trousers and his even more baggy suit coat.

He resembled a wizened, lined, shrewd little monkey. The stage, which was supposed to leave town at five o'clock and almost never got away that early, had three passengers. The last man aboard had hurled his flower-print carpetbag to the man atop the coach, had glanced once up and down the roadway, then had climbed inside with a pearl-handled sixgun butt showing as he bent over to climb aboard.

The gunguard got settled, the whip whistled up his hitch and the stagecoach horses leaned into their collars. Frank Tillitson sighed as the vehicle went past, and shifted position so that he could watch it leave town at the northern end. Then he cleared his pipes, spat aside, and looked across the roadway, southward where the café was. He nudged his lanky, thin companion and they stepped down into the roadway side by side.

It was a little early for the café to be full, but six or eight local men were already at the counter when Stanton and Tillitson took seats. The caféman eyed Leo Stanton, bundled as he was, with brief interest, then nodded to both men and went after two more platters of food.

They had been eating in silence for several minutes when two burly blacksmith's helpers walked in, followed by Ben Albright. The sheriff, seeing Frank Tillitson, came down to sit nearby as he awaited breakfast. The caféman only served one kind of a meal three times each day. There was no selection. Ben nodded to Leo Stanton and watched Doc eat for a moment, then said, 'What are you doin' up so early, Frank?'

Tillitson replied without raising his head. 'Thought we'd get this over with before we came over to see you, Ben.'

'What about? It must be important to get you stirring at sunrise.'

Tillitson did not answer; he did not have to, the caféman appeared with Sheriff Albright's breakfast, and Ben immediately went to work with his eating utensils.

Leo and Frank dallied a little over their second cups of coffee, then exchanged a look, paid up and went back outside where sunlight had not yet reached, although upon the opposite side of the road it was as bright as a new copper penny.

Leo Stanton gravely eyed the outside of the jailhouse, which was about as inviting as was the inside. He looked up in the direction of the saloon, and over the opposite plankwalk where the stage company's corralyard stood, then he faced Doctor Tillitson, waiting for Frank to speak. But Tillitson was organising his arguments and said nothing. Only when big Ben Albright strolled forth, sucking his teeth and looking replete, did Frank speak.

'We want a little of your time,' he told the lawman, and the three of them walked over and entered the jailhouse office. It was chilly so Ben went to work firing up the wood-stove for heat, and when he turned to go sit at his desk there were three folded papers placed side by side atop the desk. Before looking at them he consulted his watch and quietly said, 'I can't give you a whole lot of time, Frank. I got prisoners to put aboard the morning stage, and that Montana lawman'll be along any minute.' Ben then opened and read the first paper. His expression did not change. He picked up the second paper, glanced through it, put it down and barely opened the third pardon, looked just long enough to read the third name—that of Jack Brunner—then replaced that paper atop the desk also, and

150

finally turned to gaze at Stanton and Tillitson throughout a long moment of dead silence.

Leo Stanton said, 'They're legal, Sheriff.'

Albright barely flicked a glance at the speaker, then continued to sit there gazing at Frank Tillitson. Frank braced; he knew Ben Albright as well as anyone did in Hammersville.

Ben reacted differently. He leaned back, gravely considered the three pardons from his new position, and while still regarding them he said, 'Frank; what the hell are you up to now?' in a mild tone of voice.

Doctor Tillitson had expected almost any reaction but this one. 'Like Stanton said, Ben, they're legal.'

Albright barely inclined his head. 'I know that. I can read. What are you up to?'

'They deserve a chance, Ben.'

'Bank robbers, Frank?' said the sheriff, and leaned with a slowly-gathering frown to study one of the pardons again. 'How the hell did you get the Governor of Montana to sign those things so fast?'

Stanton cleared his throat before replying. 'Mister Kenniston brought them with him, already signed.'

Ben gazed around at the skinny man inside his sheep-pelt coat. 'How did you work it? I talked to Kenniston yesterday and there wasn't anything said about pardons—just the money.' Slowly, now, Ben Albright turned his entire

151

body. 'The money,' he said softly, and riveted Frank Tillitson with a stare. 'What did you trade Kenniston for these papers, Frank?'

'The money, Ben. The nine thousand dollars Cole, Brunner and—'

'I know who stole that money, damn it,' exclaimed Albright, colour coming into his face, his voice rising. 'You mean to set there an' tell me you and Stanton had that money?'

'We—'

'How did you get it?'

Frank changed position on his chair. 'Well; we decided to help those fellers since no one else was going to . . . and Walt Schultz was out to get them killed and—'

'Frank; *how did you get that money*?'

'. . . It was in the bottom of their saddlebags, Ben.'

'At the liverybarn?'

'Yes.'

'You went down there after I'd brought them back, and stole it out of their saddlebags?'

'I didn't steal it, Ben. I wanted to help those fellers. When the liverybarn hostler said you'd just brought them in, I went down there on the off-chance the money might still be in their saddlebags. It was. So—Leo here and I figured to make a swap with John Kenniston.' Doctor Tillitson pointed toward the pardons. 'He traded . . . And Ben, he left town about an hour ago on the early stage—with the money

152

. . . And he wasn't a sheriff or a marshal, he was a policeman for a banking protective association they got up there which goes after the money first—he said—and the thieves second . . . Ben, he came down here prepared to trade like that. Leo and I were as surprised as you are right now.'

Ben Albright arose, stepped to the stove to close the damper a little, then bleakly marched back and sat down again. His stare at Frank Tillitson was unblinkingly bleak. 'I'm goin' to charge you, Frank. You and Stanton. I'm going to lock you both up and throw away the key. I'm goin' to bring you to trial for bein' accessories, an' for withholding evidence, and for . . . Damn it, Frank, you've always stuck your big nose where it's got no business. By gawd I'm going to break you to lead!' In a steadily rising voice Sheriff Albright spoke as he brought a ham-sized hand down atop the desk with resounding power. 'You're supposed to sew people up and shove pills down them. This here is *my* job! Have I ever tried to tell you how to splint a busted leg? No! But you think you can—!'

Stanton interrupted. 'Sheriff; Kenniston is gone.'

Albright switched his attention but only briefly as he said, 'Mister Stanton, I'm going to—'

'You'll need Kenniston to testify that we traded with him, Sheriff. You'll have to

153

subpoena him all the way from Montana . . . He won't return to Hammersville. All he wanted was the bank money and he got it. He told us last night that Montana would not get involved from here on.'

Sheriff Albright sat stiffly for a moment until the implication in Stanton's statement soaked in, then he eased back very gently in his chair, staring at the skinny man. During the ensuing silence they could all hear walking horses out in the roadway. That was about the only sound.

Ben Albright's anger was boiling, deep down. He continued to stare at Stanton, until he eventually said, 'What are you doing, getting into this mess?'

'I'm a lawyer, Sheriff. Cole, Brunner and Hunter are my clients.'

That revelation triggered big Ben Albright's fury. He roared at Stanton. 'A *lawyer*? By gawd since when you been a lawyer? You're a squatter out at your grand daddy-in-law's old homestead!' Ben heaved up to his feet, fists clenched. 'You're no lawyer!'

The roadway door was punched open and four men walked in out of the roadway. The foremost among them was using a cane to help himself move with. He looked at Tillitson and Stanton, then ignored them to look from a lowered head at Sheriff Albright. The way he was holding his head down, Walter Schultz resembled a bull ready to charge. He did not

154

hedge, he said, 'Ben; get those three sons of bitches out of your cells!'

Albright's diverted attention showed no lessening of his fury at Schultz's command, but he stood a moment regarding the other man before moving or speaking, then he said, 'What did you say?'

Schultz repeated it, and gestured with his cane to leave no doubt as to what he meant. 'Open that door and fetch those three outlaws up here out of your cells!'

Albright was like an oak tree. He did not move, he stood staring at Walter Schultz, ignoring the three tanned and tough-faced armed rangemen behind Schultz. Then he started around the desk with a roar. Frank Tillitson had one of the lanky rangemen in front of him, and when the man moved one foot back as he went into a fighting crouch, Frank shoved out a foot. The cowboy tried to catch himself, then he fell in a sprawl. Another rangeman moved ahead to get between the sheriff and Walter Schultz. He did not attempt to draw until he was moving, and by then Ben Albright was bearing down upon Schultz. Ben saw his danger and lunged, caught the man with his left hand and with his right grabbed the cowboy's drawing-wrist in a grip of steel. He was enraged, as he roared and, lifting the rangeman from the floor, hurled him against the north wall, where a bolted bench broke the man's flight.

Leo Stanton was behind the third rangeman, pushing the barrel of a nickel-plated small revolver into the man's back over the kidneys. But that rider had not started to draw, he had been too astonished at all the things which had happened in the last few seconds. When he felt the gun-barrel in his back he turned to stone. Stanton plucked away the cowboy's larger weapon and flung it backwards out through the open door.

Walter Schultz raised his cane to strike Ben Albright, and staggered as he did so. Ben had little trouble avoiding the cane as he reached for a fistful of shirtfront. Schultz staggered again, then opened his mouth wide for air, and the cane fell to the floor. Schultz suddenly fell into Ben Albright, making terrible sounds in his throat.

Frank Tillitson was on his feet, staring. He yelled at the sheriff. 'Let him down easy, Ben. Let him down to the floor.'

It was all over in another couple of seconds as Albright stepped back, allowing the other large man to crumple at his feet. Frank was the only one who moved fast now; he jumped across the man he had tripped, dropped beside Walt Schultz, speared him with one glance, then began tearing at Schultz's collar and coat. 'Whiskey,' he exclaimed. 'Ben—*whiskey*!'

There was none in the jailhouse office.

That cowboy Frank had tripped was back on his feet, gunhand gripping the handle of his holstered Colt while he stared at the greying man on the floor as diminutive Frank Tillitson sprang astraddle of Schultz, placed both hands flat down over the ailing man's chest, arms stiff, and bounced down very hard.

Schultz gasped, fought for breath, and for a moment it seemed that he might succeed in getting it, then his body quivered. Tillitson tried again to hammer breath into the cowman. He kept trying. Finally, without a sound inside the office, and with all the sudden, frantic movement stilled, Frank got off Walter Schultz and leaned his head against the downed man's chest. He remained like that for a long while before coming up very slowly to rock back on his heels staring at Schultz's face.

The silence ran on until another rangeman stepped into the doorway with that pistol dangling from his fingers that Leo Stanton had pitched out into the roadway. It was Red Barton. He looked at his employer on the floor, looked elsewhere, then entered the room and shouldered past the three staring cowboys to stop above Frank Tillitson, staring downward. In a shocked voice he said, 'Doc . . . what happened?'

Frank was still regarding Schultz's grey, at-peace features when he replied. 'Too much, Red. It was just too much. I've been giving him pills for years and telling him he couldn't keep on like he was doing.'

157

'Is he dead?'

'. . . Yes, he's dead.'

Ben Albright extended a big hand to assist Frank in arising. They did not look at one another until Red Barton had leaned down to satisfy himself that his employer was indeed dead, then the sheriff looked at Red and the other rangemen and said, 'Get out of here. And stay out of here.'

The three cowboys obeyed, shuffling out into the roadway sunshine, but Red Barton turned back at the door. 'What about him?' he asked, pointing to the dead man.

'Fetch a wagon to town,' answered Albright. 'You can take him back to the ranch and bury him.'

Barton stood a long while in the doorway gazing at the dead man, then he turned and joined the other rangeriders out where their horses were tethered at the jailhouse rack.

Leo Stanton kicked the door closed. The moment there was no sun-brilliance coming in, Walter Schultz's grey colour was no longer very noticeable, but his flatness was; a dead man had a flatness to him that had no counterpart among the living.

Stanton felt for a chair and sat down. He was still holding that small nickel-plated revolver in his right fist, apparently unconscious that he was still gripping the weapon.

Frank dusted his knees and looked up at the

158

sheriff. 'I warned him. If I've told him once I've told him fifty times he couldn't keep on like he was a healthy thirty-year-old . . . Hell; you might as well try to reason with an ox as try to reason with Walt Schultz.'

Albright turned away from the dead man, went to his desk-chair and eased down. He was wringing wet with sweat. He had moved faster, had felt more anger, and had met the climax of all the trouble with more pure astonishment than ever before in his life. He leaned on the desk, saw those three papers still lying there, considered them over a period of hush and stillness, then reached for the keys and wordlessly arose and went over to the cell-room door. After he had disappeared down through there, Leo Stanton said, 'I need a drink, Doctor.'

Frank slumped onto the wall-bench over across the room. 'Have one,' he replied. 'Just one, but go ahead and have one. You shouldn't, and you know that, but by gawd you earned the right. Go on up the road and have one, Leo. Then ride on home or you won't reach there until after dark and your wife'll be worried. Go on . . . This mess is all over. Go on, do as I say.'

Leo Stanton departed, still wearing his sheep-pelt coat although it was really hot in the roadway now. He remembered at the last moment, as he was going out the doorway, that he was still clutching the little revolver, and

159

regarded it as though someone had thrust it into his hand. Then he said, 'I never carry guns, Doctor. Never.' He dropped the little weapon into a pocket and disappeared out through the doorway.

When Hugh and Jack and Cal entered the jailhouse office they stopped dead in their tracks staring at the corpse of Walt Schultz. Jack was the first to speak. 'What happened?'

Tillitson answered. 'He had a heart seizure and upped and died right there.'

Albright went after their hats, handed each man one of them with their personal property inside, then he went to the desk for the pardons, and as he passed them out he said, 'Get out of Brulé Valley and don't never come back. Never, for any reason under the sun.'

The three partners looked at the pardons, then over at Albright, mute but beginning to comprehend.

Frank Tillitson blew out a gusty breath and glanced at the astonished three men holding those papers in their hands. 'The lawman from Montana made the trade and I gave him back the money. You're free, each one of you.' He forced a feeble smile. 'You're never to return to Montana, but otherwise you can go wherever you like . . . Boys . . . no more banks, no more holdups of any kind. I'd like your words on that.'

Hugh was gazing at the medical man. He said, 'You got it. You got my word, Doctor.'

160

Then he also said, 'I'm sorry for Mister Schultz.'

As Jack and Cal were also making promises Frank turned to stare at the corpse again, and when he spoke his voice was different; it was crisp and had echoes of irony in it.

'You might want to remember something, boys. Look at him; he had money and influence and a huge cow outfit, but he never overcame wanting to bully and harm people . . . And there he lies, as good a sign that there's a law of retribution as you'll ever see if you live to be a thousand.'

Ben Albright went out into the sunbright roadway with Hugh Cole, Jack Brunner and Cal Hunter. He regarded them stonily for a moment before gesturing southward in the direction of the liverybarn. 'You got plenty of daylight left. You can be ten miles on your way before sunset.' Ben struggled with the words but finally got them out. 'Good luck . . . and remember; don't ever come back.'

Jack re-set his hat and squinted against the unaccustomed sunglare as he led the way southward, still clutching his pardon signed by the governor of Montana. When Cal caught up he said, 'By gawd, that's hard to understand.'

Brunner kept walking. 'Don't try; if that old bastard hadn't died on that jailhouse floor like that, Cal, he'd have had his men all around out here when Albright kicked us out . . . and *we'd* be flat out.'

161

At the liverybarn the dayman blinked, then scuttled after their rested horses without waiting to be ordered to do so.

Fifteen minutes later they were on the westerly road out of Hammersville, and in the hazy distance was that same pass where they had been captured in their bedrolls about a week earlier. As they rode toward it Hugh Cole settled both hands atop his saddlehorn and looked at his friends. 'Now what?' he said. 'No point in heading for Mexico, and we dasn't turn back toward Montana.'

Jack really did not care, but he said, 'California? I've heard they got some fine big cow outfits down there. And it don't snow very much.'

Cal had his reins looped, rolling a smoke. 'They got gold out there. I met a feller once in Great Falls who showed me a nugget on his watch fob he got out there.'

Jack sighed. 'Just as long as it don't come from a bank,' he said, and Hugh Cole made one of his rare smiles.

We hope you have enjoyed this Large Print book. Other Chivers Press or Thorndike Press Large Print books are available at your library or directly from the publishers.

For more information about current and forthcoming titles, please call or write, without obligation, to:

Chivers Large Print
published by BBC Audiobooks Ltd
St James House, The Square
Lower Bristol Road
Bath BA2 3SB
UK
email: bbcaudiobooks@bbc.co.uk
www.bbcaudiobooks.co.uk

OR

Thorndike Press
295 Kennedy Memorial Drive
Waterville
Maine 04901
USA
www.gale.com/thorndike
www.gale.com/wheeler

All our Large Print titles are designed for easy reading, and all our books are made to last.